MARK
OF WAR

MARK
OF WAR

NEIL SWINDELLS

authorHOUSE®

AuthorHouse™ UK
1663 Liberty Drive
Bloomington, IN 47403 USA
www.authorhouse.co.uk
Phone: 0800.197.4150

Published by AuthorHouse 10/13/2015

ISBN: 978-1-5049-9262-6 (sc)
ISBN: 978-1-5049-9263-3 (hc)
ISBN: 978-1-5049-9264-0 (e)

Print information available on the last page.

Any people depicted in stock imagery provided by Thinkstock are models,
and such images are being used for illustrative purposes only.
Certain stock imagery © Thinkstock.

This book is printed on acid-free paper.

Contents

Chapter 1 1

Chapter 2 7

Chapter 3 19

Chapter 4 29

Chapter 5 39

Chapter 6 47

Chapter 7 57

Chapter 8 65

Chapter 9 75

Chapter 10 83

Chapter 1

It was the branch of that tree in the Malaysian jungle, channelling the drip of moisture that landed with monotonous regularity on his face that kept him awake. Ten long hours later, buried deep in the leaves and branches he had pulled over him, he heard the enemy patrol approaching.

They were, as all his training had told him, excited and totally terrified. Silence was his weapon. Even on that soft carpet of leaves he could hear their footfalls and counted them through. Just six, the last one – the wireless operator? - struggling to keep up.

Were there more? Mark Ryham waited. Not a sound. Now was the time to move.

Hand over his target's mouth, the six-inch blade went into the heart with surgical precision. Mark lowered the boy's body gently to the ground and slid back into his own green grave.

The patrol, eyes strained to the front, moved on, totally unaware that one of their comrades lay dead on the jungle path behind them and other phantoms lay in wait for them.

The ambush was swift and deadly; almost balletic in its precision. This was one enemy patrol that would not reach its target - the wire perimeter fence of the bumpy airstrip where RAF transport planes stood ready to fly home the National Servicemen who has finished their term, and bring the next generation of tremulous young men to face life at the sharp end of action.

Back in the jungle, Mark waited for the natural sound of birdsong and the drip of tropical rain to return, before sliding from his hideout, crawling out to retrieve his victim's radio pack, and setting off on the torturous tree-to-tree trail back to camp. There, he knew, the mission would be seen as a triumph but he felt no elation. This had been his seventh killing in a war he hardly understood. Those before had been in fire fights at long range where the victims were almost anonymous; "Kill or not be killed," as the training manual had it. Now he had blood on his hands. It was not a comforting feeling.

Mark already knew that certain members of his unit thought he was "soft" when it came to shooting to kill. This had arisen in a stake-out across a river when Japanese riflemen had hidden themselves in trees to fire on approaching British troops. Brian Riley, Mark's "spotter" – the man with the binoculars – had pin-pointed a would-be sniper to the left of their field of action. Through his telescopic sights, only just developing at the time, Mark could clearly see this target. He whispered to Brian, dug deep into the leaves about six feet to his left: "He's about fifteen years old. He can't even climb trees. He's hanging there like a gibbon. If I fire now, all the others will spot where we are and we'll have a hell of a salvo. Do we know that everybody else is under cover?'

Even before Brian could reply, a shot rang out from the right of them, followed by a burst of bren gun fire, which scattered the would-be snipers like a flock of pigeons. Mark had not altered the position of his rifle. His "gibbon" was still firmly in his sights. With icy precision, he shot the trigger hand holding the gun, and his target fell from the branches.

"He won't be firing again," he said to Brian. "But at least, he's still alive." Then they slid backwards through the leaves to take turns in carrying the wounded back to camp.

Two weeks later, Mark was nursing a pint in the mess when two military police arrived. "Major Hadley wants to see you," said the one wearing the three stripes of a sergeant. "We're to take you under escort." And so, Mark, before finishing his beer, was marched down to the nondescript building which passed as Company Headquarters.

Major Hadley appeared to be a quite elderly man for his rank. His iron grey head was bowed over papers on his desk which Mark surmised to be his own personal records. That patrician head lifted and the major said: "Bringing back that radio set was a commendable action, but from what some of your colleagues have reported, it appears that you have your own ideas of how we should be fighting this particular war?"

Mark paused before he replied. "In the time I've been here, I've killed seven men. I do not believe, with all I know about the two world wars our own country went through, that destroying the young men of Malaysia, or even Japan, is going to help them one bit."

Hadley paused before he quietly asked; "You're a Christian?" "Well, yes, I went to a Church of England school, sang in the choir, but I like to think I was a responsible journalist before I joined up. Reporting Remembrance Services, as I did for several years, did make me ask questions."

Hadley studied the papers before him, and said: "I see you completed your journalistic apprenticeship before joing the army when you were twenty. You've served five years and are due for discharge very soon." Mark: "Yes. Next week." "You know that because you've done regular service and not National Service, your former newspaper does not have to re-employ you?" "Yes. But I was hoping to move on to a daily newspaper rather than a local weekly anyway."

There was a long silence. Then the major said: "Because of your attitude to killing, I believe you could be the certain type of man we are looking for. I have a proposition for you. If you say no, not a word of this conversation must ever be repeated outside this office. Understood?" The last word came like a shot from a rifle. Mark, stiffening in his chair, immediately replied: "Sir!"

"Right," said Hadley. "As an intelligent man, you will know that we and the Americans are engaged in what our politicians like to call a 'cold war' with Russia. We know for a fact that there have been some attempts to infiltrate American air bases in East Anglia. It's small beer at the moment, but we wouldn't want it to get any stronger.

"I can arrange an interview with Colonel Wilson, editor of the Ipswich Daily News, who is one of us. You will, to all intents and purposes, be engaged as a general reporter, but the colonel will direct you to specific operations, which will require all your undercover army skills and the ability to disappear, sometimes for weeks on end. If it becomes vitally necessary to 'despatch' somebody, it will be legally correct to do so."

Mark: "You mean I get some sort of licence to kill?"

Hadley smiled for the first time. "I wouldn't call it anything as glib as that, but, essential, yes. However, with your record and attitude, I'm can't imagine we are going to have a game shoot! What do you say?"

Mark: "I'm in."

Five minutes later, he was back in the mess. His unfinished pint stood exactly where he had left it. There were few shifty expressions on the faces of the men around the table, but most of them gave him a warm welcome.

"No jankers, then?" said Brian.

Mark grinned. "No, it would have cost them too much to keep me locked up. I've been sentenced to going to Nancy to be measured for a demob suit!"

This remark brought a roar of laughter around the table. His companions knew that he was referring to the rather effete young man who took especial care measuring their inside leg measurements for uniforms. They also knew that the provision of a demob suit for ex-soldiers had long disappeared.

"Okay," said Mark. "I'm out next week. I'll buy you all a drink."

Chapter 2

The flight home was hardly luxury class. They slept on the floor of that battered, long-service transport plane, their heads resting on their over-stuffed, and not exactly comfortable, kitbags. Mark had changed into his best uniform but many of his companions had opted for their battle gear. Some sort of statement on their service? Why not?

Farewells at the landing base were brief. Suddenly, these young men who had fought and seen others die beside them, were home. Their little war was over. They had families and perhaps still-faithful girl-friends to see. They were off.

It was only when Mark, travel warrant secure in the top pocket of his uniform, arrived at Mark's Tey to take the familiar train to Sudbury, that he finally felt the transition in all its enormity. No more jungle. No more hour-on-hour danger. Just the tranquil vista of early summer Suffolk. Early barley, already bright in the fields. Wheat still green.

As he relaxed back in the faded seat of the sturdy old steam train as it trundled over the magnificent viaduct at Earl's Colne, he mused on he journeys he had made the other way when, the only male in a class of 42, he had been taught shorthand and typing at the Colchester Polytechnic. Had he attempted to chat up any of those 41 girls scribbling away and touch-typing to the solid beat of the large baton wielded by the draconian mistress before them? No, he hadn't. He just boarded that train, and went home.

Drifting gently into Sudbury, Mark was surprised to see the amount of new houses. Then he recalled the classic quote of a Sudbury councillor at the last meeting he had reported, when it was announced that it was about to become an overspill town. "Those Cocknies will be coming down Ballingdon Hill eating fish and chips, and we can't stop them!" His prophesy had been correct.

Sudbury Station was exactly as Mark remembered it: solid red Victoian bricks, gray slate roof: that wonderful reminder of the steam age before the politicans decided that that the arrival of the car had made local stations, and the local branch lines, no longer necessary. The Stationmaster was not wearing his top hat, a wonderful bygone tradition which Mark had mischievously recorded when he had reported Mr Parlant's arrival several years earlier. But Mr P bore no grudge. He greeted Mark with a firm handshake and a sincere welcome home. Mark smiled broadly and thanked him, recalling perhaps that, apart from his top hat, Mr P had three delectable daughters – although, of course, he had no idea if they had all been snapped up in his absence.

Mark was still smiling as, kitbag on shoulder, he walked up Station Road towards the Free Press office. He was wondering whether he should just drop in to say hello, when a a pleasant female voice said: "You're looking mighty pleased with yourself." It was Mrs Groom, just that bit older but still as attractive as Mark remembered her. Mark thrust out his right hand but Mrs Groom laughed and said: "That's not a homecoming!" She grasped him by the shoulders and planted a lip-sticked kiss on both cheeks." His kitbag, packed to Army regulations with boots at the bottom, landed with a thump on the pavement. "I hope everybody else is as pleased to see me," said Mark, and returned the kiss, minus lipstick.

When he got his breath back, said: "Tell Frank I'll be round to see him. I need a car." Mrs Groom smiled and said: "I'll make sure you get a bargain." She turned, and tip-tapped elegantly on her high-heeled way.

Mrs Audrey Groom went back some way in Mark's memory. She and husband Frank had caused quite a stir in the still rusticated market town when they had arrived from London to take over the car service station just around the corner from the Free Press office, especially when Audrey, always prettily dressed and frankly sexy, decided she would help out by driving one of their taxis. There was no shortage of customers, invariably male.

As Mark, kitbag restored to his shoulder, moved on, he remembered when a cameraman from the Free Press's sister paper at Bury St Edmunds had been called in to cover a particular assignment and had Mrs Groom to drive him. Arriving back, somewhat late, he pitched stones at the Editor's window. When the sleepy head of Mr Lewis appeared, the snapper shouted: "I've bonked Mrs Groom!" Mr Lewis curtly replied: "Well, don't tell anybody else. Without their adverts, we'd be bust." And slammed the window down. That particular photographer never covered another story for the Free Press.

The recollection probably persuaded Mark that he should call in to his old office. Mrs Bunce was still there at the front desk, greeting visitors and taking small ads. "Alow Mark, ow are yer gitting on?" Five years gone and it was still "yisterday" to to the true Suffolk Mrs Bunce.

"Hello Mrs B," said Mark. "I've come back in one piece. I was just wondering if I could say hello to Mr Lewis if he's still here."

"Oh yis," said Mrs Bunch. "A bit has changed but he's still here. I give him a buzz." She picked up the telephone. "Young Mark is here. He'd like to say alow." There was a pause, she replaced the phone and said: "Gu on thru."

Mark opened the door to the room where he had typed up so many lists of those who had attended funerals and some, not many, more exciting stories. There was a young man on the telephone and two girls hammering away on the old upright typewriters. "Oh well, something's changed. They've got women here now," thought Mark as he walked through.

Mr Lewis had hardly changed. Perhaps, Mark thought briefly, if you lose your hair early, a bald man is a bald man. End of story. "Hello Mark," said the non-ageing bald man, rising from his desk. "How are you?"

"I'm fine," replied Mark. "I'm not here to give you trouble. I know that I've been away too long to be re-employed. I just wanted to say hello and ask for a little advice."

Mr Lewis relaxed in his chair. "It's so nice to see you. They were great years when you were here. How can I help you?"

Mark paused for a moment, then said: "I've a new job. And it could be quite risky."

Mr Lewis, suddenly removed from his daily fare of council meetings, Women's Institutes and flower shows, straightened up in his chair. "Go ahead."

Mark paused. Then he thought: "Here's a man I've known for several years, Totally British. Totally dedicated in all the things I believe in. I'll risk it. "I'm off to see Colonel Wilson in Ipswich," he said. "Give him my regards," said Mr Lewis. "You know him?" queried Mark. "Yes, we work together."

Mr Lewis straightened in his chair. After several seconds of thought, he said: "Mark, I've been through two wars and served in the last one. If there is going be anything like a third, then I'm totally with you . . . and Colone Wilson. And I promise that not a word of this conversation will be repeated outside. I wish you the very best of luck."

"Thank you," said Mark. "I bumped into Mrs Groom on my way here." ("As most people do," Mr Lewis muttered very quietly.") Mark chuckled. "Yes, well it was quite a warm welcome home!" Then more seriously: "I'm on my round to the garage to see if Frank can fix me up with a car."

Mark's old editor relaxed into his chair. "I can remember teaching you how to drive in the firm's old car. Now what was it? Oh yes, a Morris Minor!"

"Yes," said Mark. "And great tuition it was. Knowing how to drive got me out of all sorts of problems in my army days."

"How was that?" asked Mr Lewis. "Well" replied Mark, "when I promoted to corporal, later sergeant, I was issued with a Jeep – I'm not sure why, but the other lads thought it was terrific. I could ferry them down to various places they liked to visit."

"And what sort of places were they?" asked old serviceman Lewis, with a half-smile on his face. "Well, they were mostly bars but one or two places were of - now how should I put this? - of rather dubious character."

"You mean brothels?" "Well, yes, but should the Ministry of War ever interrogate me on this, I'd be able to honestly say that the chaps spent much more time in the bars than the other places." Mark paused, then added: "But then, I suppose when you are eighteen, as most of these lads were, sex with a professional doesn't take long, while you can linger over a pint or several."

Mr Lewis laughed. "I think your reading of the human character, especially that of the male, is excellent." They both rose, and shook hands again. "Now, off to get your car. And don't let the bastard cheat you!" They were the words that resounded in Mark's ears as he closed his ex-editor's door.

He fondly said goodbye to Mrs Bunch as he left the office, walked down that familiar street, turned left and strolled across the traffic-free street into the car showroom. It wasn't Frank who greeted him, but Fred, an old friend of his schooldays. No handshakes this time. Just a big grin on both faces.

"Hello Mark," said Fred. "We thought we'd lost you when we didn't hear anything!"

"No," said Mark. "Only the good die young." They both laughed. "Well, we should have known." said Fred, then, putting on his symbolic salesman hat, asked: "Is there anything I can do for you?"

Mark looked around the showroom, then replied: "Well, I need a car. Nothing special. Just an ordinary car that everybody is driving around."

Friend Fred laughed. "Well that's something different. I thought I was going to sell you a Merc or a Jag!" Now Mark laughed. "I didn't make that much money in the army. I just want something I can cruise around in so the local bobbies don't think I've nicked the mayor's silver!"

The friend now quickly became the car salesman. "Well," said Fred, "we've got a Morris Minor which will cost you £631 or a Ford Popular test car for £390. They say that unless you have the suspension of a Minor greased regularly, the front wheels can fall off! But it has never happened as far as I know."

"Fine," said Mark. "Let's go and look at the Ford."

It was probably the most boring car he had ever seen. But apparently it was selling by the thousands. And it was just what he was looking for. "I'll have it," he said, pulling his wallet from his back pocket.

Fred was impressed as the required notes were dropped in his outstretched hand. "Well," he said. "Whatever you say, you seem to have made a few quid." "Well, don't tell any of the other buggers, "said Mark. "They'll expect me to buy all the drinks!"

Mark drove his Popular, with its approved full tank of petrol, out of the garage, and parked, very carefully, under the Gainsborough statue on Market Hill. Years before, he had been sent out to find a girl-friend he could kiss on this very spot to make a front page New Year picture for the Free Press. Mercifully, thanks to the huge overcoat he had started to wear, and the modesty of the girl, neither of them was recognisable. But the picture worked.

By some strange move of fate, as Mark, now tall, bronzed and acne-free, stepped out of his modest Popular, who should he see but Marianne, that very girl of his yesterdays. But she wasn't a girl now. She was an elegant woman, immaculate hair, make-up applied to perfection. Mark walked over and said: "Hello Marianne." She turned. Saw who it was, threw her arms around him, reached and planted a lingering kiss on lips.

"Jeez," said Mark. "This has been some home-coming. Mrs Groom and now you!" "That old bat!" snarled Marianne. "I hope this was better!" "By about thirty years and the fact I've thought about you every day while I've been away," said Mark. There was a long silence. Then Marianne said: "Take my arm, Sir." Mark did so, and they walked gently up North Street before turning into an impressive shop showing ladies dresses, costumes, and, discretely, far back in one corner, under-garments.

Marianne disengaged from Mark as they walked in. "Could you find us some tea, Betsy?" she said the a young salesgirl, who immediately scurried off to door at the back. Marianne ushered Mark through an altogether more impressive door in the centre of the showroom. She didn't go to the imposing desk immediately before them, but sat on an elegant sofa to the left, patting the seat beside her. Mark sat down.

"This is my empire," she said, simply. "I have smaller shops in Hadleigh and Haverhill, and larger ones in Colchester and Ipswich."

"How? How did this all ... "She placed a gentle finger on his lips. "Shuss! I think our tea is on it's way. I'll tell you everything when Betsy has gone." She was right. Even then, with the lightest of taps, the door burst open and young Betsy appeared with a tray, teapot, milk, sugar . . . even biscuits . . . cups and spoons. "Well done, Betsy," said Marianne. "Thank you so much." Betsy bobbed, and disappeared.

As they sat nursing their cups of tea, Marianne begun. "Life wasn't easy in those years after we all left school. I know it wasn't great for boys having to go into the Army or whatever, but there wasn't any real direction for girls. My parents didn't want me to go into the silk factory where most of my friends were stiching away. So I hung around with nothing in my pocket, while they at least got a few bob. And then I saw an advert in the Fress Press for a girl assistant in this dress shop. I dressed up as best I could, applied, and got accepted."

"I'm not surprised," said Mark. "I'd have thought anybody would have snapped you up the moment your appeared!" Marianne half smiled. "Thank you for the compliment, but it didn't quite work out like that." "I'm sorry," said Mark. "What happened?"

"You're not going to believe this, but Mr Baristowe, who owned all this, was a randy old bastard. He didn't want somebody to sell his dresses, he just wanted to get into her knickers. I told him to bugger off. After quite a long time, he called me back and asked me to marry him." "And you did?" asked Mark. "Yes," said Marianne. "It didn't last long. He popped off. I hadn't exactly worn him out, as you can imagine. But I was left with all this!" "Good for you," said Mark. "You don't think I was wrong?" "No, no, no! Let's face it, you and I were born with f-all. We had to find our way. And you did."

Marianne relaxed, placed a hand on his, and asked: "Have you got anybody special?" "In my sort of world," he told her, "there's very little time to have any sort of relationship, especially a special one." "What do you do?" demanded Marianne. "I can't tell you because that would put you in danger." "Christ!" exploded this new Marianne. "Let's go to bed, Mister Bond!" "You see too many pictures!" laughed Mark. But he didn't say no.

Their encounter was explosive, but brief. It was several minutes before Marianne ran a gentle finger down his face. "You said you thought of me a lot while you were away. Can you tell me why?"

Mark pulled her close. "Those years at the youth club. Those dances. You must have known I was crazy about you? I even got into fights over you! When I was in the army, you were my comfort blanket. I'd kill people, see people killed around me, fall into some poxy foxhole and dream of you before more bullets would start tearing up the turf above us. Marianne. Marianne. My guardian angel."

"Hardly an angel" said Marianne. "If I ever get back here," said Mark, "I'll still fall at your feet."

Chapter 3

Mark didn't leave Sudbury immediately the next day. After his night with Marianne - and a a good Suffolk breakfast of eggs, bacon and fried bread, cooked by her own fair hands, he drove down to Market Hill and parked. He walked across the road on the right-hand side of the that long square leading up to the Gainsborough statue, and stepped into the offices of S. Pearson & Son, Solicitors.

Nothing had changed in this staid, beautifully panelled Victorian office, except that yesterday's dragoness at the reception desk had been replaced by a younger woman, who actually smiled as Mark approached. "Hello" he said. "I'm Mark Ryham. I was hoping to have a quick word with Mr Pearson senior if he's not too busy."

"Could I just ask if this is any legal problem that you may have, or anything else?" asked the receptionist, with a light accent which Mark couldn't immediately place. "No" said Mark."I've been away for some time and Mr Pearson was an enormous help to me when I was a youngster on the Free Press around the corner before I left. I'd just like to say hello again."

The young lady rose from her desk. "Please to take a seat," she said, pointing to the chairs opposite her desk. "I will go and speak with Mr Pearson."

Mark didn't sit down. He strolled to the office window over-looking Market Hill. The town was just coming to life as he remembered it. Martin's, the newsagents and general stationary shop was busy, the five permanently out-of-work old men were sitting on the steps of the Gainsborough statue rolling their last fags before they collected their dole at the office behind the Town Hall. "Mr Pearson is happy to greet you," a quiet, accented voice came from behind him. "Come this way, if you please."

It was the construction of the sentences as much as the accent that intrigued Mark as he dutifully followed this mysterious but undoubtedly attractive girl from one office to the other.

Mr Pearson had been a seminal character in Mark's career. Legal clerk to the scattered police courts that Mark had reported in his earlier years, he had also generously provided a seat in his car to those courts. On the trips back to Sudbury, he would painstakingly explain why certain judgements were made; why certain miscreants were jailed or fined, while others were sent away with a stern warning that: "If this happens again, you will . . ." What knowledge of the law, and certainly the local application of the law, Mark owed to this man.

Mr Pearson had obviously aged, but not that much. He still exuded the positive presence that had politely but firmly directed the Colonel Blimps who invariably presided over the rural courts on those days. It was only after Mark had moved to London that he had sat in a Press box recording the judgements of a woman – a firm but undoubtedly kindly Jewess. But it was just at a juvenile court. Even in the busy, still smoke-filled metropolis, emancipation of that degree had yet to arrive.

They shook hands and Mr Pearson settled into his handsome but hard-backed chair. "So Mark, you're back safely?" Mark chuckled. "Yes, I survived what they threw at me."

"And you're glad to be out of it all?" said Mr Pearson, as more of a statement than a question. Mark paused, then said: "Well, I'm not exactly out. As I've just told Charlie Lewis, the top brass were convinced that I'd make a good member of the Intelligence Service. Which is why, apart from wanting to thank you for the help you gave in the past, I've dropped in now."

The expression on the face of this venerable solicitor did not change in any way. "I can't say I'm surprised. While I knew you had the makings of a good journalist, I always thought you wanted to do, rather than report what other people had done. But, at the time, I put it down to your age. I even thought of inviting you to join us here and train in the law, and then I thought a loose cannon like you would cost us all too much!"

Mark couldn't help laughing. "That loose cannon description is much too near the truth. That's exactly what I've become, in more ways than one!" He reached inside his jacket, produced his automatic pistol, and placed it on the desk.

A startled Mr Pearson threw himself back in his chair. "For God's sake put that away!"

Mark quickly sleeved his gun. "I'm sorry. That was really was too dramatic." But the bells of suspicion were chiming – especially after meeting Mr Pearson's receptionist. Just how much should he tell him? Keep it simple seemed the best option. "I'm here to stop any possible threats to American air bases in East Anglia by whatever means. I don't believe that this will come anywhere near here but I desperately need contacts who could call me at the Daily News if they had any knowledge of anybody who might be involved. I know that, for a solicitor, confidentiality is essential, but this is a national priority."

He sat back in his chair. Then said: "I'm sorry. That must have sounded enormously pompous."

"Not at all," said Mr Pearson, who appeared to have regained his composure. "If I can help, I will." And then: "It's certainly more interesting for solicitor than defending somebody on the bicycle riding at night without showing to the rear a red light!"

Mark chuckled, then said: "I couldn't help but notice that your new receptionist has a very interesting accent. "Oh yes," replied Mr Pearson. "That's Ishkia. She's Russian. She and her family came over here just after the war. Her father has been running a bottling business up Cornard Road for years."

"A bottling business?" queried Mark. "Yes, anything you want, beer, wine, spirits . . . whatever. It's been a real success and employs a lot of local people."

"Ishkia's a very beautiful girl," said Mark. "With a successful dad like that, she must be chased by every young lad in town!"

Mr Pearson coloured slightly. "I've tried to warn her off from all that sort of thing. Nicely, of course." "Of course," said Mark, thinking: "He's probably tried it on himself. Who wouldn't?" Then he rose, and thanked Mr Pearson for sparing him the time. "I'm off to Ipswich to see my big boss now. I know you'll wish me luck."

"I certainly do," said Mr Pearson. "I certainly do."

x x x x x x x x x x x

It was a gentle drive to Ipswich. A few lorries, a bus, and the odd farm tractor trundling from one field to another. Not many cars, but several Ford Populars, which left Mark feeling highly pleased with his choice.

The Daily News offices faced the river docklands, with a handful of moored steamships and several barges plying up and down, their rusty red sails billowing in the breeze,

Mark parked opposite the offices, walked across the street and mounted the two large granite steps leading to the entrance hall. No beautiful receptionist here, nor a dragoness. A portly gentleman, wearing a dark uniform worthy of the doorman of a five-star hotel (minus the top hat) greeted him. Mark gave his name and said he had an appointment with Colonel Wilson. The uniformed man carefully studied a large, leather-covered register on his desk, solemnly nodded, and said: "I'll let them know you are here." The desk telephone, Mark now noticed, must have installed when the building was erected in the 1920s. But it worked. "Mrs Burrows. I have a Mr Ryham here to see the colonel." Slight pause. "I see, I see. Thank you."

The uniformed man turned to Mark. And suddenly grinned. "It will be a couple of minutes. I'll show you up. Welcome to the Daily News. I'm George. I was one of the colonel's sergeants in the war!" Mark reached over the desk and shook a still solid hand. "Glad to meet you George. I was a bit worried there."

"I know, I know. It's all a bit of a pantomime here. But that's how they want it; that's how it works. Sometimes I think I never left the Army! But the Colonel's a really good man. He looks after people. Mrs Burrows, who'll your will meet upstairs, is a widow of one of the chaps. She was only a girl when it happened. Now she keeps them up there in order," he added, pointing to the ceiling above him where Mark could hear the tapping of typewriters in the news room. "It's not always easy, as you'll know, but she does."

George was certainly right in his assessment of Mrs Burrows. As they walked into her office, passing two giggling girls who appeared to be far more interested in Mark's arrival than whatever should have concerned them on their desks, she came to greet them – quite tall, bobbed blonde hair, and wearing what Mark, from his cursory reading of he fashion pages, guessed to be a "New Look" costume suit: tight but below-the-knee skirt and elegant buttoned jacket. "Hello, Mr Ryman," she said. "The Colonel's ready to see you." And then: "Thank you George." Mark half expected the old sergeant to salute, but George smiled, nodded, did a gentle full-turn and strolled out.

Colonel Wilson was not quite as Mark had expected. While there was some grey hair, he looked younger, thinner and altogether more agile than any of the ex-colonels Mark had ever met.

Without any preamble, he leaned forward in his chair: "Now, you've got the short straw. We've already lost two agents on this mission and the Yanks are useless. First, they don't take it seriously, then they want to do it all themselves, and then they screw it up!"

Mark took a deep breath, then said: "I've worked with the Americans a lot. And I admire them. But I've never quite worked out, when they do get things wrong, whether it's the size of their population, the mighty dollar or a change in their perception of the colour of the young men who could be expendable."

The Colonel didn't respond immediately, and then said: "That last point about the colour?" "I could be wrong about this," said Mark, "but when I was a small boy in the war, my father drove a lorry for a local mill and delivered to American air bases. In the school holidays he'd take me with him. As a humble delivery man, he was allowed to have breakfast in the mess used by all the black servicemen, and you can imagine with wartime rationing, just what I thought of all that wonderful grub!

"I remember Dad asking some of these blokes, who always gave us a wonderful welcome, what sort of action they had seen. They all laughed and one of them told him: 'They don't let uz go into action. It could mean some of uz could end up as boss man. And that ain't howz it is in the States. Soz wez cooks and cleaners, an' look after the whities jus' like wez would back there!"

"Well, it's changed now," said the Colonel. "Yes it has," replied Mark. "You see more stripes on arms were there weren't any before, and if the US gets dragged into another war as the defenders of the world, I'm sure there will many more of my black expendables on the front line."

"Sadly, you are probably right. Now, have you any thoughts on how you can get into American air bases to see if this Russian threat really exists?"

"In my few days here at the paper, I've discovered that lads in the editorial section and a few of the inkies run a large dance band on their free Saturday nights. The only people who can afford a big band these days are the Americans, and that's who they regularly play for.

"I play the trumpet and had my own band years ago. I'm a bit rusty, but sitting up there, I would have plenty of time to observe what's going on." Then, as an after-thought: "In my experience, a dance floor exposes more about relationships than anywhere else I know."

"It certainly appears to pop up in an unfortunate number of divorce cases!" said the Colonel. "Should I mention your plan to somebody to fix it up?"

"No," said Mark. "I'll get to know the chaps, then slide in." "That sounds rather like a homosexual tactic," said the Colonel. Mark appreciated the joke. And added one of his own. "Not in my case," he said. "Although, from everything we've heard or read over the last few years, there does appear to have been a rather serious penetration in that area!"

The Colonel smiled. "You mean Philby and MacLean?" (These were two members of the notorious Cambridge Five who had fled to the Soviet Union in 1951 after passing on MI5 secrets for years). "Yes," said Mark "and the others are still here and apparently moving in very high circles indeed."

"I'm assured that the MI5 has closed that particular door," said the Colonel. "Yes," replied Mark. Then earnestly: "That's why I believe the Russians will have changed their *modus operandi*. They'll have gone back to root level They'll have agents here recruiting the ignorant, the innocent and the under-paid."

"It's an interest diagnosis. What now?" "I'll go upstairs, find my seat in the dance band, and report back, Sir!"

Chapter 4

Upstairs, Mark's request to sit in with the Daily News band was received with open arms. "You couldn't have arrived at a better time," band leader Gary Ross told him. "One of our chaps has just chucked it in. Apparently his new wife didn't like him being out on Saturday nights. We really need another trumpet – the Yanks have all been brought up on Stan Kenton. They love the big brass sound!"

"That's for sure," said Mark. "I played with a really ropey pick-up band at Bentwaters, and when all three of us in the brass section managed to hit the high A in the Ted Heath arrangement of Walking Shoes at the same time, you'd have thought we'd hit a home run or whatever it is that gets American rocks off."

Gary laughed, then asked: "Where do you live?" "I'm in a bed-sit down in Felixstowe. But I have a car. I can get to wherever you'd like me to be."

"Bill Summers, our drummer, lives down there" said Gary. "He can give you a lift."

And then, very quickly: "I'm sure you're a very good driver. It's just that keeping to just a few cars, I know everybody is going to turn up. We used to have a band bus, but then chaps moved all over the place so it didn't work." Then he smiled ruefully. "I don't know whether it does now. Only the other week a few of them decided to have a few pints and turned their car over with the double bass strapped to the top. It was smashed to smithereens. We explained to the GI running the gig, and he said: 'No problem.' He took us into a room where there were dozens of basses, and said: 'Help yourself.' And Joe did. He's got a bass now that would cost you an arm and several legs over here. But that's the Americans for you. *The Boys* have got have whatever *the Boys* might want!"

"Okay," said Mark. "I'll talk to Bill. And hope we don't turn the car over on the way!"

Sitting up there on the bandstand, Mark had the perfect view of the dance floor. Just one problem. A trumpet player hadn't turned up and he found himself with all too much to do, but there was a plus. Half way through the long evening, when quite a few of the older members of the band needed a pee or a drink, tenor-player Gary moved up to him and asked: "Can you play any small group stuff?"

"I taught myself listening to the Gerry Mulligan quartet," said Mark. "I know every note of Chet Baker." "Sounds good," said Gary. "Let's give it a go."

Gary went down to the microphone at the front of the stage. "Now, it you want to dance really close, we're going to play some small group stuff." He turned to Mark. "What?" "My Funny Valentine … with vocal." "What? Voice as well?" "If you want to get them back, you've got to give them something sexy." "And you're sexy?" "No, but the words are." "Okay, let's hear it."

Mark moved down to the front of the stage with Gary with his tenor sax, and the bassist.

Drummer Sid picked up his snare drum, brushes and chair, and came down to join them.

Mark raised his horn, counted the rest of the group in, and then, very softly, played the iconic tune. Then he moved to the microphone, waited for the gentle repeat opening on Gary's tenor and sang those first, poignant words: *"My funny valentine, Sweet comic valentine, You make me smile with my heart. Your looks are laughable, unphotographical, yet you're my favourite wotk of art..."* Just as he knew it would, it worked. All those local girls who had dressed and made up to look their very best, suddenly found themselves in the arms of those dreamy, wealthy (they certainly hoped) GIs.

There were two girls that Mark immediately recognised. One was Ishkia from Mr Patterson's office in Sudbury, and the other her friend, whose name Mark didn't know. They didn't need any romantic song to find them partners. While the other girls, now hungrily hanging on to their Yanks, had been sitting unhappily on the side benches, these two had been swanning around in the centre of the floor, held close by partners who had appeared to be queuing up for the privilege. They had also disappeared at regular intervals with one of the Americans, returning after ten or fifteen minutes to find another eager partner.

After the last waltz, Mark cased his trumpet and walked over to Sid, busily packing his drum kit. "I won't need a lift back," he said. "I'm going to cadge a lift on the C and C bus". Sid laughed. He knew that first C was an extremely rude word while the second simply stood for Carry. It was the bus especially hired by the base to bring in the local girls. "On the pull, are you?" he said, still chuckling. "No," I just want to know what the local girls know about those two ." Sid glanced in the direction to which Mark had nodded. "Oh, the two Ruskies. Yes, they're here every Saturday. The other girls hate 'em."

Mark managed to find himself a place on the long backseat of the bus, girls pushing up to make room for him. The bus started. After about five minutes, the girl on his right, about sixteen and clutching a plastic handbag on her lap, said tentatively: "We haven't seen you before?" "No. I come from Sudbury. I've just got a job on the Felixstowe Times." The older girl on his left said: "I hope you're not going to write about us!" Mark laughed. "Well, I don't know what you've been up to." Now both girls laughed, "That would be telling!" said the older one. But now they were happy, relaxed, smiling.

Mark gave it a couple of minutes, tucking his trumpet case firmly under his feet, then said: "I was wondering about those two down there." The reaction was instantaneous. "They're a couple of right slags!" exploded the older girl. "Outside with the blokes all the time!" Mark turned to the younger girl. "I don't know," she said, then colouring slightly: "I was outside with Jeff, and saw 'em. They weren't snogging or anything. But they were real smarmy. I heard them say things like 'You must be real 'portant in a big place like this'. And the Yanks took 'em down to the hangars and showed 'em the planes and boasted 'bout all the bombs and things they had to load on to 'em." She paused. "I don't know what happened then. I was too busy keeping Jeff's hands off of..."

"Good for you," said Mark. Then turning to the older girl, he asked: "Do they live in Felixstowe?" "Oh yeah," she said. "They live with a old man – I don't know if his their dad or anythin'. He doesn't seem to do anythin', but he must have plenty of money. He's got a grut owd boat that he keeps down aginst the Bawdsey ferry. And there's some old gal they olus goo to see in Hamilton Road."

The next morning, Mark dropped four large pennies into the slot of a public telephone and called the Colonel, who replied instantly. "Mark, Sir. Two girls at the dance last night, possibly Russian, spent most of their time persuading the GIs to show them the planes and missiles they work on. They live with a man who has a large boat. There's also an elderly lady they see regularly." There was a short silence. "Come and see me," said the Colonel. And the call ended.

Mark drove up to Ipswich. No formality now. Sergeant George grinned, and waved him through. The beautiful Mrs Burrows was equally receptive. "Hello Mark. Nice to see you again. He's expecting you."

The Colonel didn't beat about the poverbable bush. "Right," he said, as Mark sat down. "We know about the man, but didn't know how he operated. Now we do, thanks to you. The elderly lady is Mrs Siddons. She was a schoolmistress and a member of the Communist Party in the early Thirties when it was thing for intellectuals to flirt with as a new direction of society. Most of them grew up when the Soviet Union backed Hitler at the start of the last war, but some didn't. And she was one of them."

He paused. Then: "Any ideas?"

Mark thought deeply. "If he really is a Russian agent, I could arrange a boat accident that would take him out. But it's that boat that worries me. He's hardly tripping to Russia with his secrets, which means France, Holland or Norway. If we chop him too soon, we break the chain. I think we should liase with the intelligence guys in Europe before we do anything drastic."

"Good thinking," said the Colonel. "I'll put a watch on that boat. Now, what about Mrs Siddons?" "You can leave that to me," said Mark. "In a gossipy small town like Felixstowe, it shouldn't be that hard to flush out any equally elderly sympathziers still around." "Right," said the Colonel. "I'll leave it to you. Keep in touch." "Sir!" said Mark as he rose, and left the office.

Outside, he passed the two girls still cluttering away on their typewriters, and paused at the next desk. "Thank you Mrs Burrows." "Don't call me that," she said, standing to face him. "I'm Rita." "Well, thank you Miss Hayworth," said Mark. Rita laughed. "Well, my dad did go to all her films, but I had an aunt called Rita. It's sort of a family name."

Mark looked at this slender blonde before him. In for a penny, in for a pound? Why not? "Rita, if you haven't got somebody you're rushing home to see, could I ask you for a drink or dinner or something? I'm totally on my tod here. I don't supposed it's changed much in the years I've been away, but a little local knowledge would be a great help."

"The Globe in Dock Street down there (she waved a hand) is still the best place to eat," said Rita. "I haven't got anybody at home . . . but I'll have to go home to change. We girls still have to look our best on our first date!" Mark laughed, then said: "Should I book?" "Oh no, they're never that busy . . . we'll turn up like Mr and Mrs Swanky and they'll give us the best table!" "You're my gal," said Mark. "What time?" "Seven thirty to eight, depending what time I manage to get out of here and titivate," said Rita. "Okay. I'll meet you there."

Mark had a bath and grinned into the bathroom mirror as he found himself shaving for the second time that day. "Taking this seriously, are we?" he said to himself. He pulled a military tie and a crumpled, but clean, white shirt from his kitpack, and an even more crumpled suit jacket. Happily, he had quite automatically placed the trousers beneath his mattress the night before. While not Army standard, the creases were quite reasonable. "Hardly Mr Swanky," he thought as he left the room, "but I might just about pass muster."

Mark stood outside the Globe. It reminded him strangely of The Swan in Sudbury where, in his local newspaper days, he had (expenses approved) treated the new Mayor of Sudbury to lunch. His guest was then the proprietor of the biggest household business in the town – as indeed his father and grandfather had been before him. They had effectively, with that badge of office around their necks, ruled Sudbury Town Hall for at least four decades.

The Town Hall? Oh yes, there were other memories there. Before his military service, 18-year-old Mark had been playing there for an RAF Association dance on New Year's Eve. Just after midnight, when the band had played Auld Lang Syne, and were about to pack up, the organiser came to the microphone, and said that they had been given an extension by the local police, which meant dancing could go on to one or two o'clock. To give the band a rest, he added, he himself would entertain, playing the banjo while his wife sang "a few George Formby songs".

This didn't exactly excite the younger dancers in the hall. Almost as one, they left to go to the bar. But there was one, a girl with beautifull red hair, who said mischievously to Mark as she passed the bandstand: "I'm taking a walk down to the river."

Mark recognised her instantly. It was Wendy. When Mark had belatedly gone to senior school in Subury, Wendy, a year older, was just about to leave. She had smiled at him over the fence that separated the girls' playground from that of the boys, and said: "I really fancy you!" They'd hardly seen each other since.

Mark walked down to the river. Wendy was there. "I'm glad you're here," she said. And pulled him to her. She undid her blouse, exposing the bra behind it. Mark didn't know what to to do. "Come on, come on," she said urgently. "Touch me." It was little more than a teenage fumble, but Wendy knew what she wanted and Mark did his best to oblige. Rather more expertly, she returned the compliment.

Mark's musings were interrupted by a gentle hand on his sleeve and a quiet inquiry: "Shall we go in?" Rita looked stunning. Her nylons, tight, plain green dress and the light summer jacket around her shoulders, set off her figure to perfection. Just how she had managed to create a new, almost regal combed-up style out of her blonde, bobbed hair, Mark had no idea. "Hello, Mrs Swanky," he managed to stutter. "Yes, let's go in."

They were given a good table, in the corner of the diningroom. Mark took the intermost chair. "Exactly right," he said softly to Rita. "Whether you are a reporter or a spy, you have to able to see whoever else is around you."

A personable young man arrived carrying both the menu and a wine list. "Thank you," said Mark. "Then: I don't want to call you waiter. What do they call you when you're not working here. The young man smiled. "I'm Roger," he said. "Thank you for finding us such a nice table, Roger," said Mark. "Give us a couple of minutes, and we'll be ready to order."

"You do have your own way of operating," said Rita, as a young man, still smiling broadly, moved away. "Make the small friends," said Mark, "and they lead to bigger ones. But it's always the small ones who really help you out when things get tough. They don't have issues; bigger pictures. It's just you, them, and your friendship."

"So where do we go from here? Is this just one of your friendship things? asked Rita, after they had ordered and steamings plates were before them. Mark toyed with his knife and fork, then said: "You are one of the nicest women I've met for a good while. At any other time I would be chatting you up like mad. But now . . . I could be dead tomorrow. I couldn't put you though that."

Rita wiped her lips delicately with her table napkin, and said: "I'm a war widow. We had one night together before he left and never came back. Don't you think I'm owed just a little fun now?" "Only if you put 'I had a little more fun with him' on my tombstone!" said Mark,

Oddly, after the warm-up chat, their love-making was mutually gentle, each waiting for the other to respond. They could have been a long-married couple. Mark slept well and awoke to the bracing smell of breakfast frying in the kitchen. He slipped into his pyjamas which, he couldn't exactly remember why, were in a crumpled heap beside the bed. He went downstairs. Rita at least had a dressing gown over her nightdress. He put his arms around her. Rita deftly moved her frying pan away from the heat, and turned. They kissed. "I'm sorry last night wasn't one of burning passion," he whispered. Rita instantly removed herself from his embrace and returned to her frying pan. "Pour youself a cuppa," she said, nodding to the teapot. "And one of me." Mark did as he was told.

Nothing was said as they tucked into their breakfast. It was only when the last crumb of fried bread has disappeared that Rita sat back and said: "Last night was perfect. I know I'm a widow but I'm practically a virgin. Just one night. Since then I've hardly played around. Just once, and it was horrible. Just bang, bang and thank you mam! But you? It could have been the first time. Just I'd always dreamed it would be."

This was confession time. "I had a few fumbles when I was a youngster," said Mark. "Just one all the way. But the lass made all the running. When I was in the army, I spent most of my time keeping my chaps away from naughty ladies. I didn't even get an invitation from a certain officer's lady, who appeared to believe that introducing young men to her bed would save the British Empire."

Rita laughed. "Come here, she said. "Let's have a virgin's delight!"

Chapter 5

At a quarter to nine, Mark walked with Rita to her office. George was already there. He gave Mark a wink, which he returned (small friends, best contacts). They joined Rita's secretaries and the Colonel in the lift. "Give me five minutes, then come on through" he told Mark.

In the office, Mark smiled at the girls as they settled at their typewriters, and asked: "did you have a nice evening?" "Oh yeah!" they responded in unison. "What did you do?" "We went to a trad band concert," replied girl number one. She turned to her companion: "What were they called?" "Chris Barber." "Oh yeah. After the first tune, lots of people started jiving in the aisles and we joined in. Then two blokes split us up and took us for drinks and things. It was great!" "It certainly sounds like it," said Mark.

The Colonel smiled as Mark entered his office, waved a hand, and said: "Sit youself down." Then, looking at the papers on his desk: "It appears that our European allies would be quite happy to see our man removed." Then, with a faint smile, "Especially the Germans." He paused. "I'm being unfair. With most of the American this side of the pond still based there, and the Russians still in Poland and the other Balkan states, you can well understand their concern." He paused. "Well, it's our concern as much as their's. After all, most of what's left of the British army is still stationed in Germany!"

"I'll go down to Felixstowe," said Mark "and do my best to arrange a tragic accident for one man in his boat." "I'm sure you will," said the Colonel, dryly.

Mark drove down and and stopped in the haphazard car park by the Bawdsey ferry. The ferry had already left but, sure enough, just up from it's berth, was a large motor vessel.

Head down, Mark settled back into his seat. After about half-an-hour the two Russian girls appeared, carrying shopping bags. They walked up the gangplank, and tapped on the cabin door. It opened and a man's head appeared. He took the bags, and with scarcely a word, closed the door behind him. The girls left the boat and took the sandy path back to the town.

Mark was relieved. His violent plan for exterminating the man and the boat had not included the girls. Not for any whimpish or sexual reasons, but purely because, firstly, he had no idea how deeply they were involved, and secondly, they could lead him to other more positive conspirators.

As the evening drew on, Mark struggled out of his clothes and pulled on a wetsuit – not the most easy operation in a small car – then slipped out, sliding quietly down to the bank of reeds behind the boat. He waited and waited as the sun went down. When it was almost dark, he suddenly felt the presence of somebody behind him. He lay still, gently unsheathing the dagger at his waist, then threw himself around, grabbing this anonymous intruder by the waist. "Mark, Mark! I'm your back-up!" squealed a femine voice. Mark exploded. "Christ! I could have killed you." "I know, I know. I'm sorry. The colonel sent me down here, in case you needed any help."

Mark looked at the young woman beside him, also in a wetsuit. "Okay. This guy usually pushes off after the last ferry of the night gets in. I'm going to let him start up, dive in, bugger up his rudder and watch him smash into that iron pier up there and hopefully, explode. If it doesn't work, I'll get onboard and take him out by hand."

"What can I do?" "If it all goes wrong, you come in and finish the job. Don't worry about me. Then you check on those girls. They're the ones who are going to lead us to the rest of the network." Mark reached into his wetsuit and removed a slim sheaf of paper. "Give this to Gary at the Daily News." She read the opening lines. "There was tragic accident in Felixstowe yesteday when a motorboat struck a metal pylon close to the Bawdsey Ferry pier. The helmsman, and believed owner of the craft, died in incident, and the police are urgently asking anyone who may have known him to contact them."

She waved it back to him. "No," said Mark abruptly. "You give it to Gary. I may not come through this, but you're going to stay out of the line on fire. If those girls look liking coming back, stop them! They mustn't get in the way."

Mark waited. The sun was going down as the last ferry arrived and discharged its small number of passengers. He waited . . . and waited. The engine on the motorboat spluttered into life. He slid into the water, clutching a hank of strong wire, and swam within touching distance of the vessel's stern. The drive propellor was already sluggishly turning but the rudder blade was steady. Mark wound his wire around it and tightened it as best he could, holding a a hefty part of it in his right hand.

He surfaced briefly for a quick gasp of air, then sank again as the motorboat moved off. Straight ahead at first, then, gathering speed, a turn to port. Mark, flippers now pressed to the boat, counted to three, then threw all his weight on the wire in his hand. The rudder swung violently to starboard. There was a splintering crash as the motorboat struck the pylon, followed by the explosion that Mark had anticipated He found himself clutching the rudder as other debris tossed around him. He unwound the incriminating wire, and flipped back to the reeds by the bank.

People had already gathered. "Nobody could have survived that!" Mark heard a woman say. "No," said another. "We'd better call the police." But the police – at least, the local bobby, was already there. Mark, head just above the water, watched him tentively step into the shattered remains of the boat and lift the limp hand on its lifeless occupant.

He waited until until the crowd, the ambulance and the police had disappeared, then, now very cold, slid from the reeds. A gentle voice said: "I thought you might need these," and a female hand passed him a towel and his shoes and clothes. It was the girl the Colonel had sent as his back up. "Thanks very much," Mark said rather brusquely, turning his back, towelling himself down and, as quickly as possible, pulling on his clothes. "Did you check the girls?" "Yes, that's all taken care of" she said. Then, very positively: "Job done?" He turned to face her. "Only part of it," he said. "But it's a start . . ."

They drove back to Ipswich in Mark's modest car. "How did you get down here," he asked her. "Oh, I came by train." "Still saving the pennies, are they?" She laughed. "That's funnier you think," she said. "My name's Penelope but everybody calls me Penny. They certainly saved a penny or two on me. They didn't even book me into anywhere to stay. I sat out on the front all night, holding my case!" She nodded to the small overnight bag on the backseat.

"Christ!" said Mark. "We'll find a hotel or something." Then, just in case she thought he was trying something on, added very quickly: "Somewhere you can freshion up. We both need something to eat anyway."

The Old Oak was more of a pub than hotel, but it had a large sign announcing rooms and food. An elderly couple, probably the landlord and his wife, were behind the bar. Mark said: "We'd like something to eat, but could my friend here use one of your rooms for a little while? She's been rushing around for hours."

The mature lady lifted the heavy wooden flap in the bar, walked through and said: "Cum along a-me, gal," and led Penelope away. "I'll have a pint," said Mark. "Yew up from Felixstowe then?" asked the barman, waiting for the froth on Mark's tankard to subside, then topping it up. Mark nodded as the beer mug was expertly slip across the bar. "Hear there's been some sort of a do there. Some poor bloke hitting the quayside and blowin' himself up."

"There seemed to be a lot of policemen around when we left," replied Mark. "But we didn't know what it was all about." When Penelope returned, he quickly told her: "It seems there was some sort of nasty boat accident in Felixstowe. A man died. That's why we saw all those coppers as we were driving out."

"Oh dear," said Penelope. "It's so sad when these accidents happen."

They ate quietly in the timbered dining-room, probably once the saloon bar in the drinking heyday of a previous time. "That was lovely," Penelope told the elderly landlady as she came to remove their plates. Running her hands down her large but spotless apron, she told them: "I git some help when we're busy, but in the quiter times, like today, I do the cookin' . . . and the waitressin'!" "It was really nice," said Mark, sincerely. "We'll always know where to stop when we come this way again."

Back in the car, he said: "I love places like that. For me, it's what England is all about." Little did he know, wthin a couple of decades, with the smoking ban and the commercial ambitions of international breweries, villagers would be desperately campaigning to save their local pubs.

"Thank you Penelope. You've been a great backup." "Come on," she said. "You can call me Penny." "No," said Mark. "Penelope is a beautiful name. The Colonel is getting on. He'll be getting his seat in the House of Lords soon. Then the person who knows most about the operation – that's you – should be in line for the job."

"A woman? No. It's not going to happen."

"Why not?" queried Mark. "We've had women MPs for years, there were great women foreign agents during the last war, women writing best-sellers, doctors, actresses, singers . . . what makes you think women can't move up a gear?" He paused.

Then said: "It has to be Lady Penelope when you take the ermine."

Penelope laughed. "They warned me you were a charmer. But you're really a calculating bastard!" Now Mark chuckled. "Calculating, yes. But a bastard, no. I can assure you I know the names of both my parents, and they were happily married!"

Chapter 6

Penelope was sitting beside Mark when they faced the Colonel the following morning. He appeared to have every daily newspaper on his desk. He looked up after he had finished reading *The Times,* and said: "It seems to have gone very well."

"We can thank Gary for that," said Mark. "He's the local correspondent for all the nationals, and I wrote our version of what happened, which Penelope passed on to him. He's made a bob or two, but Fleet Street can afford it!"

"Well done" said the Colonel. "Now where do we go from here?"

"I'd like to go back to Felixstowe and suss out the old lady. I really think she holds the key to the whole thing. If I can watch her long enough, and see who goes to her house, we'd have a much better picture of what's going on."

"And Penelope?" asked the Colonel. "Penelope has been splendid – a real professional," said Mark. "If I can keep myself totally unobserved, we could return as a honeymoon couple, and carry on the observation."

Both the Colonel and Penelope sat back in their chairs at this suggestion. "No, no," nothing like that", said Mark. "We all know that honeymooners only have one thing on their mind. People just smile, and leave them alone. It's the perfect cover."

The Colonel and Penelope relaxed in their chairs. "Go on," said the Colonel. "There's an hotel opposite the old lady's place. It's a little way down the street, but it should give us a good view of her front door. We'll book a week ahead, and, if the bridal suite has already gone, insist on a room overlooking the street . . . because we love the sunshine in the morning! We'll turn up in our finery, me with a drooping carnation in my lapel buttonhole, and Penelope with some confetti in her beautiful hair." "Thank you sir," Penelope interposed. Mark chuckled, and carried on. "They'll almost certainly ask if we would like dinner in our bedroom, which, of course, we would – and breakfast the next day."

"Seems you've been here before," said Penelope dryly. "No" Mark replied quickly. "I've just waited at receptionist's desks around the world while this whole rigmarole has been played out. Of course, I always wished the happy couples the very best of luck."

Now Penelope laughed. "I'm sure you did, I'm sure you did." Then she asked: "What should I pack." "Oh, enough for a week, I should think. And a gun." Both Penelope and the Colonel stiffened. "A gun?" queried the Colonel. "You're expecting trouble?"

Mark leaned forward. Then slowly said: "During the boat incident, apart from the girls, I spotted a couple of highly anonymous heavies, possibly three, at the back of the crowd. They weren't interested or excited by what had happened. They were totally expressionless. They were professionals . . . probably Russians. And I believe there are more of them here. I don't want it to come to a gunfight, but if it does, we've got to be able to hit back. And that means all of us. In their game, they don't take prisoners."

The next morning, they were in the gun room in the basement of the building. Mark shot first. Three bulls, two inners and one rather wayward. He reloaded and passed the automatic to Penelope. Four bulls, two inners. "You never cease to amaze me," he said, ruthfully. "Oim a country girl," said Penelope in a mock Suffolk accent. "If yer brung up to hit a runnin' rabbit from the back of a movin' binder with an owd shotgun, hittin' a bludy grut target that don't move with one of these things (she waved the automatic) ain't that 'ard!"

"If I was worried about you before, I'm not now," said Mark. "Let's go and find our Ruskies."

Three days later – a Saturday – Mark in his hastily-purchased "wedding suit", drooping carnation, and Penelope, looking altogether better in a trim costume and just a speck of confetti, walked into hotel in Felixstowe. "Let my show you to the bridal suite," said the smiling young man at the desk, rushing round to grab their suitcases and show them to the lift. In their room, after thanking and tipping the young man, Mark moved instantly to the window. "Good" he said. "Just what we wanted."

Penelope patted the large double bed in the middle of the room. "Which side?" she asked.

"I'm not exactly used to double beds," said Mark. "I'll take the side closest to the window." Penelope opened her small case, took her toiletry bag to the bathroom, and came back to place her nightdress on the pillow on a lefthand side of the bed. As she did so, there was a gentle tap on the door. "Come in," said Mark. The door opened and a young lady pushed a trolley into the room. "These are your starters, she said, and this, (pointing to a bottle of champagne), "is with the compliments of the management." "Thank you, and thank them very much," said Mark. She placed the dishes and bottle on the table, and smoothly disappeared with her trolley.

Mark moved immediately to the champagne, removed the foil and the wire encasement, and opened it. Just a gentle fizz. Penelope was impressed. "How did you do that? Most people I know manage to spray it all over the table." "Oh, it was years ago" said Mark. "I told a French waiter how impressed I had been by the way he had handled the champers, and he let me into the secret. Always turn the bottle, not the cork. You have it let it breath a bit, but that's it."

Mark poured the champagne amd they sat down to eat. The main course arrived, followed by the pudding, a delicate concoction of custard and apples. The young waitress paused at the door after collecting their dishes, and said: "Have a sweet night."

"That was charming," said Penelope warmly, as the door closed. "But not British," said Mark, shortly. "Oh, come on, come on, why?" "We say goodnight, sleep well. We don't add the sugar."

Penelope laughed. "Have you ever been in a honeymoon suite before?" "No." "So could that be why she said what she did?" Mark paused. "I'm sorry. I'm looking for suspects everywhere. But you are almost certainly right. She's probably a drama student earning her pennies to pay for her course. Let's face it, if you're doing Shakespear, the word 'sweet' is like carrying a bag of humbugs around with you."

"Goodnight, sweet prince, and flights of angels sing thee to thy rest." quoted Penelope.

Mark grinned. "My good Horatio, if I can find my pyjamas (scrabbling through his case)

Hamlet will join you in bed!"

Suddenly, the girl who seconds before had been quoting Shakespeare, was shaking. "What's up?" asked Mark. "I'd put a bolster between us if we had one. "No, no," said Penelope, "It's not you. It's what could happen us tomorrow."

Mark eased himself into the bed and stretched out beside her, Her didn't touch her. "I know what you are going through," he said, "I shouldn't have brought you into anything like this. This is going to be nasty, There are two, possibly three, that I'm going to take out."

"You mean shoot them?" Penelope was suddenly sitting up beside him. "Yes," said Mark. "That's my job. I try very hard not to be, but I'm a professional killer." There was a silence. "And I'm your back-up?" queried Penelope. "Yes, but I don't think the Colonel knew what was involved." Mark, tall, strong and scarred, paused. "You know what I think about you. You are one of the best shots I've ever seen, but you're a lovely young woman with all your life before you. I'll do this on my own. You keep your head down."

"That's not how it works," said Penelope. "I'm your partner." There was a long silenece as Mark thought deeply. Then: "Right. Early tomorrow, I'll go out to the car. I've got an Enfield rifle there. You'll be my sniper. If I get into trouble, you can pick them off up here and blast the tyres on their car. Agreed?" Penelope nodded, then, turning away, said very softly: "I'd rather be Olivia than Horatio." Mark placed a gentle hand on her shoulder. "Another time, another place."

They both awoke early the next morning. Mark dressed and collected the rifle. He brought it up hidden under the raincoat he also collected from the car. "Once the mag's in, it's self-loading. Here's the safety catch. Just click it up and you're ready to go. It has a long-distance sight, but I don't think you are going to need that."

Penelope took the rifle, tucked into her shoulder and aimed at a picture on the wall. "It's lighter than I expected." "Yes, but it's extremely accurate and has an amazing range. I last used it in Malaya when . . . no, we won't go into that now." He moved to the window. "I'll go down. I think they're on the move."

"What are you going to do?" asked Penelope quickly. "I'm going to flash my card and attempt to arrrest them. They won't accept it, of course, and that's when I expect the trouble." He paused. "I think I had better take our cases down. Pay at reception and apologise for leaving early." Penelope laughed wryly. "I'm never to understand you. You're about to go down there and get involved in a gun fight, yet you're going to book out as if nothing has happened!" "Exactly," said Mark. "Remember,

I don't exist. I didn't book into here under my name. If I get blown away out there, the Ruskies won't be jumping up and down believing that they've nailed a member of the Intelligence Services. They'll have murdered an innocent chap on his honeymoon. Just think what the Press will make of that!"

"What about me?" asked Penelope. "You, crackshot Lady P, are going to open this window. Sit there with the rifle. And if I mess it all up, shoot the bastards. Hide the gun under your coat or something, and come down. If I'm OK, we'll get in the car and piss off. If I'm not, you call the police to take me to hospital or the morgue."

Mark left the house. He approached two men standing outside the home of the long-time Communist sypathiser, the third of his suspects having hurried down the street to collect their car. "Excuse me gentleman," he said, politely. "I'm from the British security services. Here's my card. You may have heard that there was a rather dramatic incident here yesterday. That's why I have to ask who you are, and why you are in Felixstowe."

One of the men took a cursory glance at the card, and said: "We are businessmen. This is a holiday resort which we believe is ready for expansion."

Perhaps it was the bland English accent that took Mark off his guard. As he turned to the second man, a vicous punch took him in the stomach, a second crunching into the back of his neck. He pitched forward. "Go, go!" shouted his assailant, drawing an automatic and holding it to Mark's head. "I'll get his card and finish this limey off!" It was the last thing he was ever to say. The semi-conscious Mark heard the crack of a rifle and saw blood spurting from a hole between his attacker's eyes. Two more shots rang out. And then a third. Under high revs, the car roared off leaving an ominous trail of petrol behind it.

Seconds later, Penelope, smoking rifle in her hands, was beside him. "Are you alright?" she asked anxiously. "I'm fine, thanks to you. You were brilliant! They won't get far with their fuel running out. Let's go!"

They ran to the car. "You get in the backseat," said Mark. "And let's see if we can get this bloody sunshine roof open." He reached up, turned the antiquated handle above, and the roof opened. "That's a first," he said. "British car sunroofs are designed to open in the winter, but not the summer. This must be made by a foreigner, and it works. Now you can pop up there and get a fair shot at whoever we're chasing."

"Well, I know I'll die laughing with you," said Penelope, professionally dismantling and cleaning every part of her rifle, then checking her ammuition."

"You're not going to die, if I can have anything to do with it," said Mark. "You've just saved my life. The least I can do is save yours."

There was a long silence. Then Penelope asked: "Will I ever get to know you?" "What do you mean?" asked Mark. "I know you had a little fling with Rita. And then you were off."

"Oh, come on," said Mark. "You where there. You know the Colonel said there was the problem down here. And sent you with me. What the hell was I supposed to do?"

"You know that Rita's pregnant?" "She can't be!" exclaimed Mark. "She told me she knew all about stopping that sort of thing." "Happily," replied Penelope," "she has a boy friend with almost the same hair and eye colour as you, who can't wait to marry her."

"So, I'm going to have a son or daughter who I will never know?"

"Rita is quite a romantic," said Penelope. "She told me it would never have worked because you were a warrior." "A warrior?" "Yes, her dad was a just an ordinary loving dad when the war started. He joined the RAF and died in the Battle of Britian. Her mum said he was married to his Spitfire." "Come on. I would never put myself up there with the Battle of Britain pilots!" "No, but your whole approach is to find the baddies, and shoot them down." "Okay. Now I'm some Greek or Nordic warlord." He paused for a moment, looking down the road. "They're not going to get far now as I said. Shall we go back to bed?"

"That's one of your better decisions, captain" said Penelope with a mocking salute.

Mark grinned. "That touch of military reminds me. I'd better call the local police and explain why there's a dead Russian holding up the traffic on the street outside."

Chapter 7

Making love to Penelope was an entirely new experience to Mark. She took charge. When he kissed and caressed her, she said sternly: "Not now. Not there." After several minutes of this, Mark's natural male passion had subsided. He stopped holding her. "I don't what the hell is going on here. Are you going by the book or something?"

Penelope snuggled back into his arms. "I'm sorry," she said, "but this is all new to me. And you're right. We were all told to read a certain book in our last year at the rather classy school my parents sent me too. Most of us were embarassed, but I remember one the girls saying: 'I'm only seventeen, but I could teach her a thing or two!' "Was the book by Maria Stopes?" asked Mark. "How did you know?" "I found it in the secret book cupboard at home when I was about thirteen. I read half of it, and didn't understand a word." "Neither did I," said Penelope, "except, to be very careful!"

Mark chuckled, and held her closer with his left arm. "I did read something much later. It by a Chinese or possibly an Indian writer, I can't remember which, but it was altogether more mystical and sensual than anything I'd read before." "What was it?" asked Penelope. "It's a fairy story. A fairy story!" Penelope snugggled closed. "Tell me, tell me!"

Battle-hardened Mark relaxed on the bed. What the hell? He'd been through many worse things than this before. "Gently, gently" he said to the girl in his arms. "Relax." And she did, although holding her breath for whatever was to follow. Mark placed his right hand, fingers spread, on her smooth, young stomach. "My mystic says that there were five deer seeking an enchanted lake." He walked his fingers gently down. "The deer came to the forest," he whispered as he brushed her pubic hair, and then . . . she was breathing faster now. "What, what then? she almost begged. "The chief deer, the stag" Mark said, sliding his index finger lower, "told the others: "I shall explore the enchanted lake. And he did. He dived once, then again, Then, more quickly, three, four, five times. As he emerged, he roared: "This really is enchanting, dive in now. Come quickly, come quickly!" "Yes, yes," said Penelope. "Quickly, quickly, quickly!" The last word, through clenched teeth, transmuted to a prolonged "Ahhh....."

There was a brief silence. Then Mark asked: "Better than Maria Stopes?" Penelope giggled. "So far as I can remember, she said if I ever did anything like that, or let somebody else do it to me, all my hair would fall out!" "Yes," said Mark, "And I'd go blind!" She snuggled into him, and said softly: "What about you?" "I'm OK," said Mark. "I think I better wait until I'm big and strong again". A delicate but firm hand found its way into the Z zone. "If you get bigger than this," she said, "I'll have to send for my mother and sisters to help out. Save your strength. Sister Penelope has got things in hand!"

They woke early the next morning, dressed, and had a quick breakfast. Mark was worried. "We should have followed them last night. These are professionals. They won't have waited around."

Outside, in the car, he said: "We'll go to the police station first. They might know something." In the smart, redbrick station, next to the aging courthouse with its crumbling Victorian columns, he asked to see the superintendent, or the duty inspector if the super wasn't there. The large sargeant behind the desk asked: "And who might you be?" Mark showed his identification and nudged Penelope to show her own card. The sergeant sudied both very closely, then, after studying a large ledger on his desk, said: "You called last night to report a body in the street?" "Yes," said Mark. "That's why I'm here." The sergeant nodded. "The superintendent doesn't get in until ten o'clock, but Inspector Stanley's here. I'll see if he'll see you." He left his desk, tapped on the door imediately behind him, and walked in, door closing firmly behind him. He re-emerged to say: "The inspector will see you. Come this way." He lifted the flap on his desk, and led them through."

Inspector Stanley was a young man for his rank, but Mark knew that the Police Force had been desperately recruiting university men to update its image. Having two Special Branch officers facing him could have been something of a shock, but the inspector was up to the occasion. "Now, what can we do for you?" he asked. "First of all," said Mark. "I'd like to apologise for not letting you know we were here. Unhappily, that's the form now. Too many unarmed young coppers got excited in spy hunts and got themselves killed. We were in the gun trouble yesterday, as you know, but, thanks to my partner here, neither of us were hurt. Penelope shot the Russian who was about to kill me, and we know she got a shot into the fuel tank of our assailants' car. Can you give us any information on that?"

The young inspector didn't have to refer to the bundle of papers on his desk. "A car was found abandoned in woodland two miles from here." he said. "It appeared to have two holes in the petrol tank. We don't know what happened to whoever was driving it."

"Right," said Mark. "Could you call the military police at the Bentwaters American air base, and warn them not to let anyone they don't immediately recognise, especially two stocky men in heavy overcoats, in! Or two girls they know very well, for that matter."

"What's this all about?" asked the inspector. "It's all about the Russians," Mark told him. "They're targeting American air bases. They know they can't bomb because the defences are too good, so they're trying to sneak bombs in. They've done it before, and it's worked. We've got to stop them."

The inspector called the miliarty police at Bentwaters. Very professionally, he turned away from Mark as he was doing so. Call over, he turned and said: "Okay. They're like to see you. This is your code to get throught the gate (he passed Mark a slip of paper). Good luck."

Mark and Penelope drove up to the American air base. and showed the slip of paper and their identity cards, The large white pole lifted, and they drove gently through. "What's this all about?" asked the military policeman, with so many stripes going up his arm that Mark couldn't guess what his rank was . . . but he knew this was the chap in charge. "Have you just let a car through here?" he asked. "Yes, they're delivery men. We see 'em all the time." "Okay," said Mark. "They're not delivery men, they're bloody Ruskies!" Even as he spoke, there was deafening explosion in the buildings before them. A black car suddenly appeared, a stengun firing from the passenger side. Penelope fell and Mark took a slug in his left shoulder. With his right hand, he drew his automatic, shot the stengunner and put three bullets through the driver's window. The car veered violently to the left, and overturned."Christ!" exclaimed the young whitecap beside him. "You had better call medical." said Mark. "I think we need some help."

He was in a haze after that. He remembered professionals hands dressing his wound and asking if Penelope was alright. Told she was, he passed out.

He awoke to finding a young lady nurse taking his pulse." You're fine," she said. "Fine."

Mark was awake now. It seemed a good time to befriend this girl who was looking after him so well. "What brought you to the UK?" "My Mom was here during the war," she said. "She was a nurse, I just wanted to see it for myself." "Where was she?" asked Mark. "Oh she was at some base in East Anglia – is that right?" "Exactly" said Mark. "Anything else you remember?" "I seem to remember she said something like Sudbury and Actin." "That would be Acton." said Mark. "I believe I may have met your Mom!"

The young nurse tightened her hand on his. "How? How?"

"When I was a little boy in the war, I used to go and play with my chums in the woods behind the big mansion that had become the

American hospital. We'd go down the dumps there and pick up the packets of gum and things that they were just throwing away. We didn't have any sweets or anything, so it was terrific.

"One day, there was a whole group of the nurses having a picnic. Just me and one of my mates went up to them. And they hugged us. I suppose some of them were mothers who had left their children behind them. I really didn't know. One of them asked us if we could sing. We were both choirboys, so we said we could. "Sing," they said. "Sing!" Just why I can't remember now, probably because it was the big tune of the time, but we launched into Judy Garland's "Somewhere, Over the Rainbow". You remember?" He sang: *"Somewhere, over the rainbow, way up high. There's a land that I heard of, once in a lullaby..."*

"Talk about the Wizard of Oz! After a few seconds of our piping trebles, they were mesmerised. Then in tears. They gave us the biggest box of candy we had ever seen!" "You did meet my Mom," the nurse said excitedly. "She used to tell us that story. She said it was the nicest thing that happeneded to her in England!"

Some days later, Mark and Penelope were sitting in wheelchairs on the antiquated veranda of the hospital when the Colonel arrived. "I'm sorry to see you here," he said, "but I'm terrifically happy to see that you are both still alive." He turned to Mark. "What now, do you think?" Mark paused, then said: "Penelope has been a great partner. She has saved my life once if not twice. But I don't want to see her taking any more bullets. She's going to hate me for saying this, but I think that with her experience at the sharp end of things, she should return to headquarters and pass on that experience to those coming up."

Penelope, for once, said nothing. She was expressionless as she looked at the Colonel. He said: "You've actually done my job for me, Mark. That's exactly the plan I was going to put before Miss Fairweather. I'm approaching the end of my service and there is no-one I'd rather see take over the department. And those above me agree."

Mark realised that it was the first time he had heard her surname. But he didn't use it as, laughing, he told her: "There you are, Lady Penelope, just as I told you!" Penelope wasn't laughing. "You want to see the back of me!" she said, coldly. There was a deep silence. Then . . . "You know that's not true," said Mark. "You're my lucky penny. I flip you and whichever side comes down is just as good!"

"Ahem," interjected the Colonel. "I think I'd better leave you to sort this out." And he left.

Mark painfully manouvred his wheelchair closer to hers, placed a hand on her arm and said: "Where ever you go, where ever you are, I'll always love you. However you feel about me, that's the way it is."

"Thank you," said Penelope. But she didn't return his vow of love. Practically, she turned her chair, and started to wheel back into the hospital. "Let's get this over with," she said shortly.

Their medical treatment was professional but not comfortable. Extracting bullets is never that. Penelope's wound was a clean breach in her left shoulder. Mark had a fractured collarbone.

Several weeks later, they were allowed to leave, Mark still wearing a surgical support.

"I feel okay," he said, "but I think you had better drive, just in case.'"

They had been on the road for about ten minutes when Penelope said: "I'm sorry I didn't reply when you said you loved me. But . . ." "I know, I know," Mark said quickly. "I've thought about it a lot over the last few days. We're just tied up in our jobs. We're too professional. There's no way we could get married, set up in some country cottage and have kids . . . I don't even know if you would want to be a mother. |I didn't even know your full name until the Colonel came out with it!"

Now Penelope, hands confidently on the steering wheel, laughed. "You know far more about me than any man I have ever known. And I would love to have kids with you. But I think the wedding and the idyllic cottage had better wait until we've sorted one or two things out." She paused, then added softly: "But you can still take me to bed."

Chapter 8

The phone woke them the next morning. It was the Colonel. "First of all, I'd like Penelope back here in headquarters and you're better get back to Sudbury."There's been quite an unusual turn-up there." "Anything else you can tell me?" asked Mark. "Well," replied the Colonel laconcially, "it appears that you have been there doing all sorts of nasty things!" "I'm on my way," said Mark.

Mark driving, the journey to Sudbury was swift. He drew up in front of the solid red-brick police station and strode in. "Hello Sergeant," he said the three-striper on the front desk. "I'm Mark Ryham. I hear you need me." The sergeant was serious. "We've had a couple of explosions in the town." "Anybody hurt," asked Mark, anxiously. "Mercifully not," said the sergeant. "What sort of explosions were they?" Mark asked. "They were petrol bombs, using bottles made at Mr Malanko's factory up the road. We've got Mr Malanko and two Russian girls here claiming that you told them to do it."

The sergeant took him to a large room behind him. All the top police were there, plus the two Russian girls who Mark instantly recognised, and an older man that he didn't. "What's this all about?" he asked.

The girls were excited. "That's him, that's him!" they shrieked together. Mark took a seat. Looked towards the Superintendent, and said: "I think I know what this is all about. And, more importantly, the man they think was me while we both know I was forty miles away."

"Go on," said the Superintendent. "Possibly," said Mark thoughtfully, "our Russian friends shouldn't hear what I'm going to tell you." The Super nodded and waved a hand towards a constable who promptly escorted the girls and the man from the office.

"It's a complicated story," said Mark as the door closed. "And it's been a bit of a nightmare throughout my service. The fact is, I have a virtual double, and he works for the Soviets. At first I thought they had cloned me – it wouldn't be the first time they've tried that sort of thing – and then I dug into my family history.

"My father was orphen, adopted by a lady in my mother's Suffolk village when he was a baby. At six or seven, he was sent to a Dr Barnardo home in London, but was allowed to return when he was eleven or twelve. At fourteen, he attempted to join the Army in the First World War. He used to tell us the story of a parade at Southend when the Colonel gave the order "All those under-age, fall out!" and the parade ground was left practically deserted! Anyway, he was able to join the Royal Navy when he was sixteen or seventeen."

Mark paused for breath. "And this, dear reader, is where the story really begins," he muttered to himself. But it raised a chuckle among the more erudite of his listeners.

"My father saw some service on his destroyer as a stoker and, bizarrely, a marksman – apparently they'd call him up from the stoking room to pin-point mines - towards the end of the war, and then, as he'd signed up for four years, they went up to Russia. You'll all know this was when the Soviets had destroyed the Russian fleet. The white Russians were boarding every boat that would take them to France. My father always used to tease my mother by saying he could have married a Russian princess, but it wasn't the real story."

"What was that?" came an eager voice from the back of the room. "To put it rather crudely," said Mark, "all the real crumpet had gone by the time that ordinary seaman like my father were given shore leave. But the girls who were left were just eager to find a man who would take them from what they saw, rightly or wrongly, as their crumbling world. "My father and several other matelots had sex with with one girl, and she became pregnant."

There was an expectant hush in the room.

"Several years later, after me father had married my mother and I had been born, we received a letter from the War Office. This asked whether my father had been seaman XYZ on Royal Naval vessel XYZ in Russia etc., etc. He wrote back, or rather, my mother wrote back . . . she did all these sort of things . . . that he was, and he had. Two weeks later, they received another letter from the War Office enclosing a letter from Russia.

"It was from a Russian lady who said she had a son after the "visit" of the British sailors, and enclosed a photograph which bore a remarkable resemblance to my father. She added that she had later married one of the English sailors who had decided to stay in Russia. This explains why this son was bi-lingual. He then married and had a son himself.

"This is the man the girls thought was me. Igor Czarevitch, my step-brother, a couple of times removed. He went to Moscow University – where else? - and has popped up several times during my years in the service. His similarity has been a problem. And now he's trying it again. But, I believe we could end all this nonsense."

"I don't believe for one moment that Igor isn't a spy. But our real target could be this man." he pulled a photograph from an inner pocket. There were gasps from those around the table. "I know, I know" said Mark. "Mr altogether British Mr Stanley Wilson. The man with the handsome mansion a few miles from here who hands out the prizes at the local flower shows. Lauded as an 'international businessman' – but nobody knows what business, or where his money comes from." He pulled another picture from his pocket.

On this, he had crudely but effectively removed Mr Wilson's spectacles, his smartly-trimmed moustache, and fattened out his cheeks. The similarity to Igor was uncanny.

"I believe," said Mark, "that he is related to Igor and could be our Mister Big!"

"Just a minute," said one of the senior policemen in the room. "Your story dosen't add up." He looked at his notes. "You have Igor being born in Russia?" "Yes," said Mark hastily, "but his grandfather was a British sailor who may well have decided to come home. Was he 'turned' during his years in Russia? I honestly don't know. Nor his name."

Again there was hush in the room, then the Superintendent asked: "What do you think we should do now?" "Well, I think Mr Malanko is totally innocent. He's got an English wife, his kids go to school here, and he runs a factory that has provided jobs for local people for years. The grls are different. I've been watching them for quite a time. I first saw them here in Sudbury, then chatting up theYanks at Bentwaters. They delivered supplies to the bloke I blew away in Felixstowe, and then we saw them leaving the house there with the heavy who tried to put me away before my partner took him out."

He paused. "I don't think we should lock them up. I've had a good look at the remains of the bottles they used in their petrol bombs. They were seconds . . . the sort thrown in the bin outside Mr Malanko's factory every day. The girls didn't work for him, so either they picked up the bottles themselves or were given them with the instructions from Igor."

Mark glanced around the room. His gaze stopped at a young constable sitting just inside the door. "Excuse me being personal," he said, "but are you married?" "No sir," said the young PC. "Have you got a girl friend?" Now the constable grinned. "Not really" he said.

"Last question," said Mark, smiling himself. "Can you dance?" "Yes, people think I can!" was the positive answer.

"Good" said Mark. "I'd like you to get to know these young ladies. Just nod to them when your on your beat. Then smile. After a day or two, they'll say hello. Give it a little while, then ask them if they like dancing. They will almost certainly say they do. Then you say you would like to see them at the dance at the Town Hall on Saturday night."

"What's this all about?" asked the Inspector sharply. "It's a very gentle way of allowing the people we are up against to believe they found a way inside the legal set-up in this country," replied Mark. "The truth will be that our young man there (he nodded to the young constable) will be reporting every conversation with our suspects to you.

Far from them being inside our set-up, we'll be inside theirs." Again he nodded to the young constable. "Everything. Who they see. Who they know. What they think. Where they have been. Everything. The smallest clue could lead us closer to our enemy."

The Inspector nodded. "And where will you be while this is all going on?" "I'm going to disappear," replied Mark. "This is my home town and it shouldn't be too hard. I'll give you a phone number as soon as I have one." He paused. "Before I go, do you think we could go down to the local bank and talk to the manager?" The young inspector picked up his hat, and said: "I'm sure we could."

They left the police station and walked briskly up the slight hill, passed the church, and entered Lloyds bank. The Inspector removed his hat and said to one of the girl cashiers: "We'd like to see the manager, if that's possible." She scurried away, returning moments later to take them through to the manager's office. The manager was much younger than most bank managers Mark had met in the past. "Hello Raymond," he said brightly to the Inspector. "What can I do for you?" The Inspector returned his greetings, and said: "This is Mr Ryham from the Intelligence Services who would like to ask you a few questions."

The manager rose from his chair, shook Mark's hand and said: "I'm Trevor Blackwood. What can I do to help?"

Mark was brief. "I'm here to investigate Russian infiltration. Bank records show that your branch has been processing more roubles than any in the country."

The young Trevor rocked back in his chair. "Yes. It's been great for business. My bosses are delighted. They've put me in for a rise!" "I'm sure they have," said Mark. "And quite right too. But . . . it's blood money. I know where it comes from. I don't want to ask you, but I have too. Stanley Wilson?" Trevor collapsed, covering his head with his hands. Mark went in for the kill. "Wilson has been one of the biggest Soviet operators in this country for years. He has corrupted more young people than anybody I have ever known. I was going to take him out, but (he took his gun out, placed it on the desk) perhaps you would like to provide that service?"

He waited. The young bank manager was still folded over his desk. "Of course you wouldn't" he said, curtly. Your City bosses don't care where that money is coming from." He picked up his gun. "I think you can forget about Mr Wilson and his roubles," he said, chillingly.

"That was pretty harsh," said the Inspector, as they walked back to the police station. "It was," said Mark. "And I apologise to your friend. I admire him, as I do yourself, for being where you are are at your age. I don't have to tell you, with the training you've been through, that, in this tough old world, we have to know the men from the boys. And, in my book, you are both men who will have important roles in averting a serious threat to all our futures."

They walked back to the police station in silence. Then Mark said: "I'll pick up my bag, and pop up to Mrs Baristowe's to see if she can find me a bed for the night. If you don't hear from me in the next half-an-hour or so, that's where I'll be." "Marianne's?" exclaimed his companion. "Yes, we were at school together." "Some people have all the luck," said the young Inspector. And they both smiled.

Betsy was busy in the dress shop when Mark arrived. "Hello," he said. "I'd like to see Mrs Baristowe if she's here." "I'll see, I'll see," she said, hurrying to the office door. Mark waited. The door reopened, Betsy stepping outside. "Come in," she said.

Marianne, still sitting behind her desk, was cool. "So you're back?" Yes," said Mark. "How many?" "What?" he asked. "How many girl friends since me?" "Two." "Just two?"

"Yes, the first I was practically ordering to look after, but she's happily married now, and the other was my partner at a nasty incident down in Felixstowe. She saved my life a couple of times before taking a bullet in a shoot-out at Bentwaters when I took this," he said, tapping his neck. "She'll probably be my boss soon."

"And you were in love with them both?" demanded Marianne.

Mark thought for a long time before replying. "In the life I lead now, I'm not sure what love means. Loyalty? Yes. Comfort? Yes. Support, even a bit of bullying when everything seems to be slipping over the edge. Yes."

"Hasn't that been the role of women since Adam and Eve?" She'd stopped him in his tracks. Mark thought for a moment, then said: "Okay, you've thrown the Book of Genesis at me. And, as always, you are quite right. But let's just consider. A hundred or so years ago, the Church of England, the Catholic Church, not to mention the Methodists and all the rest of the independent religions, were united in trying to establish a society where marriage before producing children was the rule. And love, love of God first, and then love of each other, became the sacrament. "Let's face it. Virtually all the popular songs of the 1930's and 40's had love in the title. And then in our time, the 1950s and Sixties. Nat King Cole's "When I Fall in Love" and the Beatles with "All you Need is Love".

"And your conclusion?" It was an altogether gentler inquiry from Marianne.

Mark smiled. "You should know by now. When ever any whispers of love creep across this battered old brain of mine, they carry the thought and image of Marianne, the love of my life."

"And will you still fall at my feet?"

Mark paused. "Dare I say there was just a whisper there. You remembered the exact words I said to you. And yes, I will . . . I do."

Marianne rose from her desk, walked across the office and locked the door. She came back, placed two firm hands on his shoulders, and said: "Thank you for your lecture on love . . . but you shouldn't put us up on some sort of pedestal. Most of we shrinking violets have our Randy Mandy moments . . ."

For once, the ever-cautious Mark reacted immediately, pulling his flies open and ripping her knickers off. Gripping her hair in his left hand, he threw her across the desk and "had" her, with all the explosive meaning of that wondeful Victorian euphemism for coitus hardly interuptus.

Eventually, Marianne opened her eyes and said: "Christ! That's the first time I've ever been raped!" "You weren't raped," Mark said sharply. "I was under orders."

There was a long silence. Then Marianne found her panties, and, very decorously, pulled them up under her desk. She sat back in her chair and said: "Yes, you were. You were. I should have known better than taking on a man of action!"

Mark smiled ruefully. "When I'm gone, which could be any time soon, you'll be able to remember your Randy Mandy moment, and so . . . whatever cloud I explode in, will I."

Chapter 9

The next morning, Mark walked down to the police station. The Inspector was there and the young constable that Mark had recruited. "Anything to report?" he asked. The Inspector nodded to the young constable. "Well, we haven't been dancing but I've chatted to them. They're very excited. Igor has told them that Mr Wilson has a very important job for them to do, and they're to go to his place at Acton as soon as possible."

"Excellent," exclaimed Mark. "Well done constable. It fits the pattern perfectly." He turned to the Inspector. "We'll give it 24 hours, then we'll go to Acton. I know the house well. I think we should alert the Army as well."

"Christ! What's this all about?"

"Stanley Wilson is a money launderer," Mark told him. "Not just roubles, but British notes as well. I believe we'll find the girls in the cellar churning out the cash. But, more seriously, he has a gang of heavies, some Russian, the others British thugs, who run the money for him. That's who we're up against."

Inspector Stanley sat back in his chair. "I'll get on to Colchester Barracks. How many tanks would you like?" Mark chuckled. "Half a dozen sharp-shooters will do. Give them my name and tell them they can get clearance from Colonel Wilson in Ipswich. I'm sure they'll know who you mean. Then, if the riflemen can get here tomorrow, I can brief them."

There was a bit of a twist the following morning. It wasn't riflemen who arrived but riflewomen, a platoon of WACs. This didn't worry Mark. It was the guns he wanted: he really didn't mind who pulled the triggers.

The lady captain saluted him very smartly; a compliment ex-Army man Mark returned equally smartly. "Thank you for coming so promptly," he told her. "If you could call your squad in, I'll tell everybody what's going on." The captain nodded, and gave the order to the corporal standing behind her.

There was one young member of the platoon but the rest, Mark guessed, had seen some action. He told them about Stanley Wilson, the girls, and the thugs who ran the cash. Then, to lighten the stmosphere, he told them: "I know the mansion well. When I was a nipper, a friend of my mother's was the head cook and bottle-washer there. She give me a mug of water or a glass of milk and, if the then owner wasn't there, proudly take me around her dominion."

This brought the smiles he had hoped for. And he carried on: "There are four good upstair windows at the back, looking into the woods. There are four similar windows at the front with an Oriel window between them which, surprisingly for buildings of that period, actually opens. Enought, anyway, to get a rifle through it.

"This a combined Army and police operation. My plan is for us to go in through the woods. I'll open the backdoor. The Inspector's bobbies will slide down into the cellar to get the girls, while I crawl upstairs to hopefully silence Mr Wilson – not kill him, he's far too valuable for that – while you come and take up your positions at the windows I have described. We want cover at the back, but the real firepower at the front. And two of you, well hidden, at the bottom of the drive. Any questions?"

"How do we know when our targets are going to arrive, and how they'll respond?" asked one of the older riflewomen.

"I've been watching them for some time," Mark told her. "They arrive at 10.30 every morning. The girls meet them, and pass over the cash. But, of course, this is not going to happen tomorrow. I'm guessing, only guessing, that they'll drive up to the house. That's when I'll use my loud-hailer to tell them they are surrounded and tell them to put down their guns. I don't believe they will. If they turn-tail, and attempt to drive back, that's when our colleagues at the bottom of the drive come into action."

The lady captain stepped up. "Any other questions?" "No mam," came the instant reply.

"Dismiss" she ordered. And they did.

Mark found a chair. The captain drew one up beside him. "I'm sorry, captain," he said. "but I don't know your name." "I'm Jane Riley. Brian Riley's little sister. You were in Malaysia together." "Brian? Oh yeah! The best spotter I had. How is he?"

"He's OK," said Jane. "He left the Army and now he runs a very successful garage business. He's married with lots of kids. He's very happy."

"I'm so glad," said Mark. "You lose track of people you went through so much when they leave the forces." He stopped speaking. And then, soberly: "I suppose he told you that I didn't like killing people."

Jane thought. Then said: "He told me about the gibbon – the lad you thought had to have a chance of life."

"Do send him all my regards, and tell him I'll call in to see him when I'm next down his way," said Mark. "Which is?" "Guildford," replied Jane.

Then she smiled. "He also warned me that you're a 'luv' 'em and leave 'em' specialist!" "If only that were true," said Mark ruefully. "It's more luv 'em and lose em'. Most women who serve with me get killed or injured. That's why I wasn't exactly jumping with joy when you and your ladies arrived." Then he asked: "Have you got to get back to the barracks tonight?" "No," she said, shortly. "We're booked in at The Swan." "Good," said Mark. "I'm there as well. I'd like to buy you and your ladies a drink before dinner." "Love them and lose them? "No. I don't think anybody will get hurt tomorrow, except me. But hopefully not."

Buying those drinks was a learning curve for Mark. While a few of those hardened Army ladies requested a pint of bitter, others went for a Double Diamond half-pint of larger, and a few for a gin and orange, almost the traditional feminine sip of the age.

Sitting on her bar stool beside him, Jane asked: "Where do we go from here?"

"Don't even ask," Mark told her. "I'm the kiss of death, Much as I'd like to shag the pants off you, it ain't going to happen!" "Well, that's telling me" said Jane. "I'm sorry," said Mark. "That's not the language of a gentleman . . . something I believe I was, once upon a time. You, beautiful Jane, are a lady. I apologise most sincerely."

"Apologies accepted," said Jane.

"Exactly. The proper response of a lady. You'll make a wonderful dowager."

"You bastard," exploded Jane. "One minute I'm lovely, Then I'm a great-grandmother!"

"It's a natural progression," said Mark. "Shall we go to dinner?"

Jane hesitated. "Before we do," she said, "would you tell me a little more about your childhood here . . . what turned you into the hard-as-nails bugger you are now?"

Mark laughed. "Thank you for the compliment, Lady Jane. As I was saying earlier, I was just a little wartime country kid. We'd find flight flares on the big heap of earth the Americans used as their firing range, and set them off in the village. Once I came home from the base with a whole chain of 8mm machine gun bullets around my neck, which my Dad, quite rightly, grabbed off me. My friend Billy and I used to put any live bullets we found in his father's wood vice, put a nail to the cap at the back and fire it by hitting it with a hammer. We did it once too often, and it brought back his Dad's shell shock from the First Worl War!"

"Go on, go!" demanded Jane.

"Well, there were more gentle moments. My other great chum was Jimmy, moved down from London to avoid the Blitz. He and his sister Violet were the result of their mother's affair with one of the Yanks, as I mentioned earlier. Anyway, some years after the war had ended, Violet, who must have been in her early teens, told me her dream was to go to America to find her father. I wrote a poem about it."

"A poem? You?" exclaimed Jane.

"I leant to use a typewriter long before I learnt to use a gun," Mark said simply.

x x x x x x x x x x x

While hardly the Ritz, the Swan had done its best. A long table in a private room where they could all dine together, Captain Jane one end, Mark at the other. His companion on his left was the youngest member of the group. "Been in the Army long?" he asked before the soup arrived. "All my life," she said. "My parents were in the Army, both of them."

"Fascinating," said Mark. "Tell me about it."

"Well, I was born in India. I had a ayah there, so my first language was Indian. Even my parents couldn't understand me! Then we moved on. I went to seven different schools before I was fourteen. They were supposed to be English Army schools but most of the teachers were from whatever country we were in."

"How many languages do you speak?" asked an intrigued Mark." "About seven," she said, thoughtfully. "But I'm a bit rusty in some now."

"How about Russian"? "Oh yes. When we were bombing around Eastern Europe, that seemed to be the language. The accent changed a bit from area to area, but I'm pretty good at that."

The soup had arrived. Mark lifted his spoon and said: "You are going to be a very valuable member of this squad. Would you tell me your name?" "I Rose Deardon," she replied. "Everybody calls me Roz." Mark chuckled. "Great to meet you Roz. Now let's enjoy our dinner."

Chapter 10

They drove off the next day, Mark's car leading Captain Jane and the WACs in their Army vehicle. Into Long Melford, sharp right to the Acton road, then another right to the back of the woods.

They parked beside a police car on a rough verge where Inspector Stanley, the constable that Mark had selected to chat up the girls, and another constable were waiting. They were wearing overalls. "I didn't want us to be too obvious," said the inspector. Mark chuckled. "Good thinking," he said. "If anything goes wrong, you can always say you're painters who've mixed up the address!"

The winding path through the woods, which Mark remembered from his boyhood, was still there, a bit overgrown at the height of the summer, but walkable. As the trees opened out towards the back of the mansion, Mark raised his hand. "We'll thin out now and keep low. I and the constables will slide up to the backdoor. When you see us get in, you move up."

Mark flicked his hand at the constables. They ran quickly to the remaining trees before falling to the ground, and then dragging themselves by the elbows through twenty yards or so of long grass.

That door was exactly as Mark remembered it. Solid. Weathered. And unlocked. They went in. Mark nodded to the policemen and pointed towards the cellar door where, as he had anticipated, minting machinery was whirring away. He waited until that whirring had stopped. Hopefully, the police now had the girls."

As quietly as possible, he climbed the servant's staircase to the upper floor. Was that magic door still open? It was. Mark slid through and padded down to the central room, the room with the Orial window, where he guessed Stanley Wilson would be controlling his illicit empire. He took a handkerchief from one trouser pocket and a phial of chloroform from the other. "Better not blow my nose on this again," he thought as he squeezed the sleeping gas into the hanky.

Wilson was on the phone when Mark silently entered the office. On his knees, to avoid any reflection in the window before his target, he crawled forward. As Wilson finished his call and replaced the phone, that highly-charged handkerchief was held firmly under his nose. He struggled briefly, quite violently, but Mark hung on. Then his head slumped.

Mark pulled his arms behind him, took a pair of handcuffs from his pocket, and locked his hands behind the chair.

Mark was aware that the door had opened. He turned to see Captain Jane and her WACs. "Ok ladies," he said. "Now the action begins. "The police have got the girls. We've got Mister Big here, and the thugs are about to arrive. Take up your positions and good luck to everybody."

Two of the riflewomen scuttled away and Mark saw them hurrying away down the drive. "There's a couple of policemen down there," he told Captain Jane. "They'll lock the gates after the car arrives. They're bloody great iron things and it would take a tank to get through them."

They waited. And waited. At precisely 10.30 am, a large black saloon car arrived and drove up the drive. It stopped abruptly as the driver or one of his companions saw the gates swing shut behind them. At least six men, all armed, jumped out."

"Drop you arms!" roared Mark in his loudhailer. "You are surrounded!" The reply was a shot through the Orial window above his head. It purely pierced the glass; not a crack or a splinter. Just an insignificant round hole. "They knew how to make things in those days," he whispered to the women around him. But they were busy. Shots rang out either side of him. Two of men fell. The others threw themselves into the car, which, with a desperate u-turn, sped back down the drive. It was a fatal move. Quite beyond Mark's knowledge, the WACs on the gates had a bren gun, the lethal, most sure-hit machine gun of the age. With deadly precision, they stopped the car in its tracks. Then sprayed it with fire. It exploded.

"I don't think we'll have any more trouble from them," said Captain Jane. "Nor do I," replied Mark. "Nor do I."

A couple of hours later, Mark rang the Colonel. "Operation over, Sir," he said. "Captain Jane and her WACs were excellent." "Good," said the Colonel. "You had better get up here as soon as you can. We're having rather more Ruskie problems on the American airfields than we expected. Your lookalike seems to have popped up again." "On my way, Sir" said Mark.

Markdrove up to Ipswich. The Colonel was brief. "It seems that Igor, pretending to be you, has persuaded the Americans that he should be allowed to provide the outer protection of their bases. With so many of their boys going home, this obviously was a good financial option. However, there could be files and other things there which would be of use to anyone who wants to blow the rest of us away."

Mark thought for a moment. "One of Captain Jane's ladies I chatted to, speaks Russian. I think she may be able to help us here."

"Go on" said the Colonel. "Well," said Mark, "I've been very impressed with the WACs since I've been working with them. If Igor is recruiting . . . and he must be trying to get his so-called "protection" team from somewhere . . . I believe this particular lassie is quite capable of passing herself as a Russian. Or an international sympathiser at least. She speaks six other languages which, I have to confess, puts me to shame."

"They're taking over the world," the Colonel said dryly. "I think they already have", said Mark. "And I don't imagine you were referring to the Russians."

The Colonel smiled. Then asked seriously: "How do we play this?" "I'll brief Roz," said Mark. "We'll throw her into the same cell as the Russian girls. She'll say she's an entirely innocent Russian girl working over here, and suddenly this has happened to her. She'll get to know them, then, as the older woman, she'll take over. She'll start banging on the cell door and demanding to see the Russian Consulate. After a day or so of this, we'll let them go. Lack of evidence. No case, as our friendly, very efficient police inspector will tell them. Once out, the girls will almost certainly contact Igor – or he'll contact them. And our girl will be with them."

"This puts one of us in rather a lot of danger, dosen't it"? "I'm not sure," said Mark. "My experience of the Americans is they don't leave much behind them when they leave. What Igor and his team are likely to be protecting, I have no idea."

"Tell me," said the Colonel. "I was wartime kid. After school, we would all run up to the Amerian base in the village. We all knew the Yanks. Some of the women did their washing, and provided certain other services that had a few of the older residents tut tutting, but I suppous if your husband has been away for years, that wasn't so surprising

Anyway. Suddenly the war was over. We kids rushed up to the base and it was deserted. Overnight Just like that. The Nissen huts were wide open. I went home with a baseball bat, a couple packets of gum and a pin-up of some film star that had been hanging on the wall of one of huts as long as I could remember. I told my mother 'the Yanks have gone.' 'Just as well,' she told me. 'When our boys get home, there are going to be a few questions asked around here.'

"And were there?" asked the Colonel. "As far as I can remember, there was only one lady who had two children while her husband was in a

Jap prison camp. But he accepted it. They had another couple after he got home, and I went to school with the lot of them."

"Back to Igor," said the Colonel. "When, with Roz's help, I find exactly what he's up to, I'll take him out," said Mark. "Assuming he doesn't get me first, I'll switch my clothes with his, push my identity card into his inside pocket and disappear."

"Isn't this a bit too dramatic?" asked the Colonel. "I don't think so," said Mark. "Igor has used his likeness to me for years, He's a Russian spy. God knows what he's done in my name. I think it would be totally approbriate."

It was a couple of days before he heard from Roz. Her call on a public telephone was brief but professional. "We're going to break in to Bentwaters tomorrow. Then go to the headquarters. He believes they will have left files behind them and told us to go through the wastepaper bins. He says the Americans are so meticulous in their typing that they'll tear a page out and throw it away, even if it was formula for the atom bomb!"

Mark chuckled. "Well done Roz. I'll see you tomorrow."

Roz was there. Bang on time. "I'll be there, behind you. We'll despatch Igor. Don't worry. I'll do the dirty business. Good luck."

Mark drove up to Bentwaters the next day, easily opened the gates, left his car in an over-grown and well-concealed parking space behind the headquarters and, once again using his well-used lockpick, entered the building. The former CO's office wasn't hard to find; the most imposing in the centre of the building.

Igor, the experience spy, was right. There were discarded files in the bins. Mark opened a tall metal filing-cabinet behind the central desk. More files. Mark extracted these and piled them on the desk, even opening one and, after a little time persuading an aging fountain pen on the desk to find its ink, added a scrawl against one entry. Then, carefully folding back the metal bars that had held the files, he stepped inside the cabinet and closed the door, pulling out his pistol and holding it in front of him.

He did not wait long. He heard the door open. The heavy treads of Igor. And the voices of the girls. There was a pause. Then once again the heavy tramp of Igor. He wrenched open the cabinet door and Mark, gun in position, shot him once, twice. That second shot was a mistake. The first bullet had taken Igor down, but the second ricocheted around the room and pierced Mark's left shoulder. Roz rushed up to him. "Are you alright?" "Apart from managing to shoot myself, I'm OK. Where are the girls?" "The bobbies were here. They've got them." "Good," said Mark. "Now, you know the plan?" Roz nodded.

The transfer of clothes went exactly to plan. "I don't think we have to go down to the underpants," said Mark. "He's been here so time and probably buys the same ones as me." Roz smiled as Mark painfully pulled on the shirt the shirt and suit he had brought with him. "I think I'll forget the tie," he said. "Let me," said Roz, and tied it for him.

"Right," said Mark. "This is where you come in. You call the Colonel and tell him there's been a gun battle and you believe I'm dead. You need medical assistance. Urgently."

"You're joking?" exclaimed Roz. "No. I disappear. That's my job. That's me down there. Mark Ryham has gone. No more. The Russians, or whoever are the next bastards queuing up to take us down, will believe that I've gone. Your job now is to tell the Colonel. With a bit of luck, they'll bury Igor, believing he is me, with military honours. End of story."

"I don't know I can do this," said Roz weakly. "Of course you can," said Mark. "You're a tough Army girl." "I'm not that tough," said Roz. Mark took her hand. "Now Rosie, dear. This is your daddy. You've got to tell a little lie for me. That nasty, nasty man has shot that nice, nice man Mark. That's him up there. We can't leave him there, can we?"

Suddenly the Army training clicked in. "Message received, Sir!" Then Roz, with slightly damp eyes, smiled, and added: "Daddy."

"There's a phone box up there," said Mark. "Now I'd better disappear." He paused. "It's been a pleasure working with you Roz. I hope we meet up again some time." "So do I, Daddy" said Roz. Then she grinned. "That will be a first!"

It didn't end there. Wounded Mark found himself back in the American hospital. His first visitor was . . . Captain Jane. "I hear you've been smoothing up to Roz," she said, sharply.

Mark raised his right arm, his left, because of his wound, being firmly held down. "Roz has been a great companion; very professional. But absolutely nothing else. In fact, she now calls me Daddy!"

The professional Jane was nonplussed. "Daddy?"

"That's the relationship, nothing more, nothing less," said Mark. "I'm the old man, and she's the kid. And I was the one who joked about calling me Daddy. And that is certainly not a Sugar Daddy!" Now even Jane laughed.

"Has Roz told you about my plan?" Mark asked. "Yes. You've changed clothes with Igor your lookalike, and pushed your identity card into his pocket. Now you want us to bury him, saying that it's you, and you disappear."

"Exactly."

"And to where do you *exactly* disappear?"

"I have a cottage quite close to the churchyard where, quote, "my remains", close quote, will be interred. It used to belong to my grandparents. They left it to me. It's very old but very comfortable. And a wonderful neighbour looks after it while I'm away." "Can I come and see you there?" asked Jane. "Or will your wonderful neighbour object?"

"She'll make you and I a 'gud cuppa tea', said Mark, lapsing into a broad Suffolk accent." She was a good friend of my granny, and decided that she'd look after me when the dear old gal had passed on. She's never once asked what I do. I slip her a bob or two, although again she's never asked. I pretend it's for some expense or other. And I give her a bottle of sherry at Christmas. That's how the folk are around here. You're are who you are, and so are they. She won't even look surprised if I take you home with me. She'll just pop upstairs and make sure there are fresh sheets on the guest bed."

Jane giggled. "The guest bed?" Mark assumed his patriarchal pose. "Mrs Drake will know that my bed is already in pristine order."

Jane was serious now. "So that's where you'll be? So again, can we come and see you?" "I'll call the Colonel, and tell him I've been buried, and see what he would like me to do now. I believe he will agree that I should disappear. So . . . I would be delighted to see you"

"What will you do, before you hear from the Colonel?" she asked. "Well, I'll probably see if I'm any better at writing poetry."

"Oh yes," said Jane. "I remember. Could I hear something?"

"So you can go back to the Colonel and tell him I'm completely off my rocker?"

Captain Jane was embarrassed. "No, no," she said. "We all read the war poets when we were at school. And wept. And thought. When I was a training officer, I encouraged the girls to do the same thing. I believed, and I still believe, that those words from the past encapsulate the very emotions that anyone going into danger today will face."

"Okay," said Mark. I remember one that, while hardly Alfred Owen, captures the feelings of the past. It's called Stars for Violet." And, very softly, he begun:

Violet was older than me,
An evacuee,
Down from London, I seem to remember,
in 1943
Or was it 42? Well any year will do

For her, those early years

Had been filled with fears and tears
For Vi that bomb-filled London sky
Had held just one message:You could die

But now, on this village road we stood alone,
No sounds from the drome,
The Yanks had gone home,
No more gum, no more cigs, no more candy bars,
But a war-free Vi looked up at the sky,
And asked: "What do you know about stars?"

Timidly, I took this big girl's hand, and waved it at the sky,
"That brightest one's the Pole Star that all sailors steer boats by,
"You can always find it if you can see the Great Bear,
"It's a straight line from those three stars at the back,
"There, there and there!"

"But that's my favourite up there. Orion the giant.
"See! Again I pointed to that mystical land,
"Three stars in a row. That's his belt.
"Once you find that, you can trace his legs and shoulders,
"And the big sword in his hand!"

Violet was impressed. "How do you know all this?" she asked.
So I told her: "Some italian invented the telescope and discovered
the galaxy and named all the stars in it. I think his name was Galileo."
Was I right? I don't know. But Violet had felt the starlight and basked.
She grabbed my arm. "I'm lovin' this, I'm lovin' this! I didn't know."

I believe Violet became a GI bride,
As so many girls did, long ago,
I just pray that she was happy
And her stars still gently glow

"That's beautiful," said Jane. "Was Violet one of your girl-friends?"
"No," said Mark. "She was the big sister on one of my best friends,
Jimmy. We went to school together, but she was always in the class
above me."

There was a silence between them. Then Mark said: "Now I'm gone.
You're going to see my coffin carried into that church. Then see it buried
deep in a good Suffolk grave. If you or any other of the ladies there,
could shed a tear or two, it would be nice."

"What's this all about?" asked Jane, sharply. "Well it's simple, when you
think about it. I believe my luck has run out. I've taken a bullet on my

last two operations. The next one could be fatal. So, I do think I should take my aged shattered frame off the podium."

"God!" said Jane. "I do think you are the most pompous twit I've ever met! Where do you think we'll be if we all 'step off the podium'. We need men like you. Hard men. Sharp men! "And then, almost to herself, thinking back to his poem: "Our own personal Orions."

The door opened behind her. It was Roz and Marianne. They came up to his bed and simultaniously kissed him.

Mark looked at the women around him, then said, weakly: "My three Musketeers. Two of you who have stood beside me through thick and thin, and Marianne, who gave me the love and encouragement when I needed it most. I just don't know how to thank you."

"You don't have to," said Marianne. "We heard what Jane told you, and you know she's right."

Mark pointedly touched his wounded shoulder. "We know, we know," said the hardened Army girl Roz. "You've got the marks. Sadly, these wars go on. But, more happily, so do you!"

Author's details

Neil Swindells has been a journalist all his working life, starting as an apprentice reporter on the *Suffolk Free Press* at 15, progressing after National Service in the Royal Air Force to the *East Anglian Daily Times*, and then to the *Paddington Mercury* in London. After marrying Mary, then working in publishing, he was transferred to Basildon where he was editor of the New Town's local newspaper for two years before joining the *Daily Mail* as a sub-editor, becoming Chief Sub-Editor and Assistent Night Editor. Over 30 years at the *Daily Mail*, he worked in virtually every editorial department, including travel writing, which took him to many countries, and producing Fleet Street's first fashion pages in colour, before spending two-and-a-half pre-retirement years as Night Production Editor of the *London Evening Standard*. His first book, *Behind the Glaze*, the life story of William Moorcroft, was well-received in the pottery world.

Mr N.C. Swindells,
Moat End Cottage,
Little Sampford,
Saffron Walden, Essex
United Kingdom
Tel: 01371 830421
email: neilswi@aol.com

Lightning Source UK Ltd.
Milton Keynes UK
UKOW01n1504221116

288281UK00002B/46/P

9 781504 992633